Dedalus Euro Shorts
General Editor: Timothy Lane

The Prodigious Physician

Jorge de Sena

THE
PRODIGIOUS
PHYSICIAN

Translated by Margaret Jull Costa
& with an introduction by Rhian Atkin

Dedalus

Dedalus would like to thank the Direcção-Geral do Livro das Bibliotecas/ Portugal & Arts Council, England for their help in producing this book.

Published in the UK by Dedalus Limited
24-26, St Judith's Lane, Sawtry, Cambs, PE28 5XE
email: info@dedalusbooks.com
www.dedalusbooks.com

ISBN printed book 978 1 910213 38 4
ISBN ebook 978 1 910213 45 2

Dedalus is distributed in the USA & Canada by SCB Distributors
15608 South New Century Drive, Gardena, CA 90248
email: info@scbdistributors.com   web: www.scbdistributors.com

Dedalus is distributed in Australia by Peribo Pty Ltd
58, Beaumont Road, Mount Kuring-gai, N.S.W. 2080
email: info@peribo.com.au

First published by Dedalus in 2016

Printed in Finland by Bookwell
Typeset by Marie Lane

The Author

Jorge de Sena (1919–78) was a Portuguese poet, critic, essayist, novelist, dramatist, translator and university professor. His opposition to the Salazar dictatorship in Portugal led to him going into voluntary exile in Brazil in 1959 and, after the military coup in Brazil in 1964, he moved to the United States. He taught first at the University of Wisconsin and, for the last eight years of his life, at the University of California in Santa Barbara, where he was Professor of Comparative Literature. Although he never returned to live in Portugal after the Revolution of 25 April 1974, Sena continued to be a critical observer of Portuguese politics. He died in Santa Barbara in 1978.

The Translator

Margaret Jull Costa has translated the works of many Spanish and Portuguese writers. She won the Portuguese Translation Prize for *The Book of Disquiet* by Fernando Pessoa in 1992 and for *The Word Tree* by Teolinda Gersão in 2012, and her translations of Eça de Queiroz's novels *The Relic* (1996) and *The City and the Mountains* (2009) were shortlisted for the prize; with Javier Marias, she won the 1997 International IMPAC Dublin Literary Award for *A Heart So White*, and, in 2000, she won the Weidenfeld Translation Prize for José Saramago's *All the Names*. In 2008 she won the Pen Book-of-the-Month Club Translation Prize and the Oxford Weidenfeld Translation Prize for *The Maias* by Eça de Queiroz.

In 2014 Margaret was awarded an OBE for services to literature.

To enter a deliberate contemplative state, all you need is to enter the state of those who meditate, namely, to walk in the grace of God, as long as you do so with no consciousness of mortal sin...

Father Manuel Bernardes
On the Contemplative State

I piss upwards at the brown skies so high and so far away – With the approval of the large heliotropes.

Rimbaud
Evening Prayer

Introduction

The Prodigious Physician is an astounding book. First published in 1966 in a collection of short stories, it would take a further ten years and a political revolution before the book could come out as a stand-alone novella in 1978. *The Prodigious Physician* weaves a tale of love, persecution and resistance, mixing traditional prose narrative with poetry and experimental literary techniques. Sena's style of writing requires our close attention, and his explorations of sexual and political freedom retain the power to challenge readers, even today.

Jorge de Sena was one of the most influential and productive intellectuals to emerge in twentieth-century Portugal. As a scholar, he was firmly committed to exploring Portugal's literary heritage with painstaking attention to detail, from the Renaissance poet, Luís Vaz de Camões, to the modernist icon Fernando Pessoa. Sena read broadly, and was an avid fan and critic of cinema, and an enormous range of influences and references may be identified in his work – not least in *The Prodigious Physician*. This novella draws not only on the two stories from the medieval Iberian collection, the *Orto do Esposo*, to which Sena himself drew our attention; it also alludes to well-known legends (such as Narcissus and Faust), to fairy tales (Sleeping Beauty), to the biblical story of Christ, and makes reference to cinema – a medium of which Sena was particularly fond.

As a politically-engaged intellectual, Sena was well aware of the possibilities of literature as a tool in the resistance against authoritarian regimes such as the highly conservative Estado Novo (New State) dictatorship that governed Portugal from 1933 to 1974. Under the regime, significant restrictions were placed on writers and artists, and self-censorship was encouraged; books deemed inappropriate could be seized after publication and the author and publisher jailed. The isolationist and authoritarian regime headed by António de Oliveira Salazar limited political opposition both in Portugal and in its then colonies through the use of a political police force (known as the PIDE, the International Police for the Defence of the Nation). Sena himself was a known opponent of the Salazar regime, and following his involvement in a failed coup d'état in 1959, he sought exile in Brazil as a means of escaping police scrutiny. When Sena was writing the novella, in 1964, he was still living and working in Araraquara, in the Brazilian state of São Paulo, although he would soon move again, this time to the USA, after Brazil also found itself in the grip of a dictatorial regime that lasted from 1964 to 1985. He never returned to live in Portugal and died in California in 1978.

The plot of *The Prodigious Physician* is misleading in its simplicity: the title character is a young horseman who is endowed with magical powers, his body having been sold to the Devil by his godmother. He cures a 'damsel in distress', Dona Urraca. The two fall in love, but their lovers' idyll is soon brought to an end by the Inquisition, which takes them prisoner on account of the horseman's alleged witchcraft. The trial of the horseman lasts for many years, during the course of which Dona Urraca dies, with the horseman eventually dying too. The final chapter of the novella sees a popular revolt finally overthrow the Inquisition's rule of terror. The devil of this story, as it were, is in the detail: *The Prodigious Physician* is a shifting tale marked by ambiguity in its telling.

In the first instance, the prodigious physician of the title is difficult to pin down. In Portuguese, the word *físico*, which, after quite some deliberation has been translated here as 'physician', is both an old word for doctor or magician, and it refers also to the physical body and to the laws of nature. The importance of the horseman's physique is repeatedly referred to in the novella – from the opening scene and his subsequent encounter with the maidens in the forest, to his continued physical beauty even when he is severely tortured. His physical relationship with the Devil (who accosts him sexually whenever he is naked and alone), and his curative powers that rely on the use of his blood, are the crux of the story and the reason given for his imprisonment by the Inquisition. Notably, the physician or horseman rejects the possibility of taking a proper name, and the ambiguity around his identity is crucial and continually reverts attention to the physical. In the first half of the novella, the physician is referred to as the young man, the horseman or the physician. In the first six chapters, he is closely associated with his horse, and the two figures repeatedly create a sexual tension. In the opening line of the novella, the two bodies are as one as they penetrate the valley (an image that will be repeated later, when he encounters the ailing Dona Urraca in chapter II). Later in that first chapter, the existing sexual anticipation is heightened by the neighing of the horse as the maidens/goddesses ogle the young man's naked body. In one grotesque scene in chapter IV, he fantasises/dreams about Dona Urraca emerging from an orgiastic scene, biting into the horse's severed penis.

The identity of this character, the physician, is more closely associated with his visual appearance than with any name or background story. For Dona Urraca and the Devil, he is the image of love and all its positive and liberating potential; for the Inquisition, he is the image of evil and opposition. Even while the physician's image is a central symbol in the narrative, it is not attached to him, as we see from the young man's fascination with his own image, and then from the superimposition of his face first onto his dead lover's face, and later onto those of his torturers. Furthermore, just as his image is understood variously by the different characters in the novella (including the physician himself), the way that he is described also changes: he is described first as 'the young man' or 'the horseman'; and by the end of the novella as 'the body'. For the most part, however, the physician is identified only by the pronoun 'he'.

The uncertainty surrounding the prodigious physician's identity is just one of many complex ambiguities that emerge both within the story and from its telling. The translator's task is made all the more difficult by Sena's deliberately confusing use of both subject and object pronouns. Margaret Jull Costa's painstakingly close attention to detail in this respect both clarifies for the Anglophone reader where necessary, and retains Sena's linguistic play where possible. The parallel narratives present two possibilities at once, while 'whirlwind' narratives and a mixing up of narrative positions (such as in chapters I, IV, V and XII) also complicate reading, for it is not always easy to decide whether an event is imagined, or is a magical interlude, or really happens within the narrative – or more than one of these options at once. Furthermore, stylistic quirks such as the parenthetical inclusion of question marks after the word 'maidens' after their sexual interaction with the young man serve to question the very vocabulary that we have at our disposal, underlining the loaded nature of certain identifying terms (p.70). The episodes which take place in the clearing in the forest are particularly tricky in this respect, and again, Margaret Jull Costa has faithfully reproduced the confusion that Sena creates and which adds depth to this story. Between them, the Devil, Dona Urraca and the physician form a kind of unholy trinity that both references and diverges from the biblical story of Christ, with the possibility of the physician's divinity made explicit at the end of Chapter V. One of the most difficult of all the complicated games of identity and narrative that this story contains is the question of the relationship between the Devil and Dona Urraca. Is Dona Urraca the Devil in another guise? And/or are her maidens yet another incarnation of the Devil? The question is never answered for certain, although many hints are given, and the reader must become a sleuth to find out for sure, noting details that will become increasingly meaningful as the story progresses (watch out for the 'mocking laugh' and the 'acrid smell' as you read).

The Devil himself is something of an odd character in this novella, for he is not particularly evil. Indeed, the rather likeable, lovesick Devil is used to draw a contrast with the nastiness of the physician's inquisitors. The plot of the second half of *The Prodigious Physician* satirises the type of political repression that Sena witnessed in Portugal and Brazil alike. The Inquisition – led by Brother Anthony of Salzburg (whose name recalls the Portuguese dictator, António de Oliveira

Salazar) – imprisons the physician, subjecting him and all of his acquaintances to a long and arduous process during which he undergoes severe torture, and his inquisitors are revealed to be reprehensibly corrupt and deeply un-Christian. Sena's work challenges assumptions about good and evil, revealing the boundary between the two concepts to be as much about perspective as it is about any inherent truth. Equally, a number of other dichotomous pairings are exposed as being much more complex and ambiguous than they may seem at first view, for example: holy/unholy, virginity/promiscuity, witchcraft/science. Even the boundaries of fictional form are shaken in this novella, as Sena uses a range of techniques, from deploying poetry within the prose narrative to emphasise particular themes (such as the redemptive powers of sexual love), to providing varying perspectives on the same event through parallel columns of text which, although they cannot in fact be read at the same time, serve at least to deconstruct a narrative hierarchy which presents one perspective as being superior to another. Throughout the book, Sena interrogates notions of sexual and political power, weaving the two concepts together and exploring the revolutionary and liberating potential of love in its many forms. The result is a story that is all the more enjoyable for the challenges that arise from its multifaceted ambiguities.

The task of the translator of *The Prodigious Physician* is decidedly difficult. She must draw on a deep and wide-ranging understanding of Portuguese and European cultures in order to understand and find the best means of conveying Sena's multiple references to, for example, the troubadour tradition, the chivalric romance, fairy tales and legends from Sleeping Beauty to Faust. She must be able to move, as Sena himself does, between the high register of medieval dialogue to the colloquial tones of contemporary speech. She must find a means of maintaining the laugh-out-loud humour of the Devil's put-down to Brother Anthony, while at the same time not foregoing the deeply sensitive critique of oppressive regimes. She must make the novella as sexually explicit in English as it is in Portuguese, while retaining Sena's use of innuendo and his linguistic coyness. And she must keep all the joy and fun in the text – clarifying its linguistic ambiguities where necessary for understanding, but keeping its many delightful quirks and maintaining the readability, ambiguity and literary prowess that make this novella one of the most challenging, and most rewarding, of twentieth-century Portugal's literary tradition. Margaret Jull Costa's accomplished new translation can be relied upon to do just that.

Rhian Atkin
Cardiff University

I

He rode down the hill, his erect body swaying in time to the horse's gait. The sun, still high, filled with crackling light the wild valley that lay spread out before his wandering, abstracted gaze, and he was utterly oblivious to the lush vegetation, the glittering tawny rocks, the small animals that fluttered, ran, crawled or fearlessly stood their ground, staring at the vast, moving mass of horse and horseman. At the bottom of the valley, the narrow, metallic strip of a river could be glimpsed intermittently between the ranks of poplars and willow trees. Still in the same absorbed, distracted mood, the horseman was now riding down towards the river, reining in his thirsty horse, which, nostrils flaring, was now quickening its pace. The murmur of the water rushing over the pebbles and the whisper of the leaves set dancing by the tenuous breeze made the horseman suddenly conscious of the heat of the day, the acrid smell of sweat and dust emanating from both him and the horse, and of how weary his limbs were and how dry his mouth. He rode on down, seeking some patch of shade where the river was at its cleanest and deepest. His gaze was no longer vague, but keen and darting, scrutinising the secret and apparently deserted places along the river bank; and his ears, equally attentive, and accustomed to accompanying his eyes on these searches, could hear no human noise above the burbling of the waters and the soft rustling of the trees. He gave a deep sigh, anticipating the long, lingering bath he would take in the river before resting in the shade. Afterwards, he would eat, then sleep until morning, when he would be woken by the birds and the chill dawn air and continue on his journey. Where to? And a smile of bitter indifference was already beginning at the corners of his mouth when the horse stopped and lowered its head to drink. He dismounted and, before crouching down to take a drink himself, he flexed his legs, as if he were still on horseback, and stretched arms and shoulders and back. Then he knelt down by the water and reached out with cupped hands. As he did so, and as always happened, he immediately had to grab his hat to stop it falling into the crystal-clear current. The hat had grown up with him and must, on no account, get wet, and yet he always forgot. Carefully setting it down beside him, he, at last, drank long and gratefully. The water was very cold, much colder than you might expect there in the valley, in the height of summer, so cold that a shiver ran through him. The water, though, was so clear that he decided, nevertheless, to bathe quickly, to wash and refresh himself. And seated now on the ground, he began to take off his boots. The horse had moved away in search of lusher grass. The young man's pointed boots were made of the finest red leather. He slowly rubbed his feet, childishly wiggling his toes as if he were about to count them. Then he got up, unbuckled his broad gold-studded belt and put it down beside the boots and the hat. His long tunic hung loosely about him, glowing white in the shade dappled green and orange by the sun. Bending down, he grasped the edges of the tunic and drew it up over his head. His long, fair hair, sticky with sweat, fell in soft disorder, and he ran his fingers through it to untangle it. Before undoing the lace tie holding up his brief undergarment, he again looked about him. Not a sign of anyone for miles around. He stood there completely naked. But just as he was about to wade into the water, his feet already wet, he heard the familiar mocking laugh he had known almost since he was a baby. And arching his eyebrows in an expression of utter tedium, he went back and lay languidly down on the fine grass. He lay there in a pose of patient, indifferent abandon, his head resting on his arms, and allowed the Devil, who was invisible, to work himself up into a frenzy of desire. Long caresses ran lightly over his skin, whispered kisses nipped his body all over, hands lingered on his crotch, a hardness pressed against him, trying to penetrate him – it had been the same ever since he had reached manhood and whenever he took off his clothes and was alone. He put up with it as he might do with an unavoidable affliction, which neither excited him nor provoked feelings of horror or repugnance. And, up to a point, he felt slightly proud that he could inspire such a stubborn, ridiculous passion, one for which, however hard he looked, he could find in himself not the slightest flicker of interest to justify it. After much furious huffing and puffing, the Devil satisfied his lust and left him alone; to bathe in the river then became an urgent necessity, as if he had become invisibly begrimed by a love to which he had been sold. For he had been sold, once and for all, when his godmother (who had given him the hat), seeing him still prepubescent, but with the body of a grown man, had summoned the Devil, who had immediately enfolded him in a passionate embrace. In exchange, he had received immense powers and, over time, had come to think that the Devil wasn't really asking such a lot of him, contenting himself with a mere obliging availability, in which he, the young man, did not participate with so much as a gesture or a tremor. He brusquely fended off a more stubbornly penetrating pressure and turned over onto his back. As usual, the poor Devil went into a frenzy of excitement, all in vain, and had to make do with a rather unsatisfactory satisfaction. Then the young man stood up, shook himself, ran his hands over his body and plunged into the water, where he thrashed noisily about. He felt perfectly happy like that: leaping and jumping or else lying down and allowing the water to wash over him, then violently scrubbing and splashing himself clean. The water wasn't so very cold, and he savoured that long, delicious bath, moving abruptly between stillness and movement, until, dripping and covered in tiny brilliant droplets, he waded back to the shore, where he stood distractedly watching his horse, who was waiting quietly for him. And then he felt hungry. He went over to the horse and took from the saddlebags a piece of bread, a slice of ham and an apple, then sat by the water's edge to eat, feeling the breeze drying his back and his hair. The sun was already getting lower in the sky and it was growing colder, so he moved into a sunnier spot where, once he had finished eating, he lay down.

… … … … … … … … … … … … … … … … … … … …

I asked the river about my love
the one who left so long ago,
and for whom I'm dying of love, ai*!*

I asked the river about my love
To tell me where he goes to bathe,
and for whom I'm dying of love, ai!

The one who left so long ago
and where he bathes his lovely body,
and for whom I'm dying of love, ai!

The one who left to go far away
And where he went to wash himself clean,
And for whom I'm dying of love, ai!

I asked the river about my love
Where he washed himself clean of our nights together,
And for whom I'm dying of love, ai!

I asked the river about my love
Where he washed himself clean of our sin,
And for whom I'm dying of love, ai!

Where he washed himself clean of our nights of love
His living face borne off by the waters,
And for whom I'm dying of love, ai!

Where he washed himself clean of our sin,
The one who left to go far away,
And for whom I'm dying of love, ai!

The three maidens came strolling along the river bank, singing a song that one of them had begun to improvise; and *With a slight puff of pale cloud that rose up from the grass with each step they took, the three goddesses, for so they* their three voices combined to repeat, with variations, the stanza that the first of them had sung. Their footsteps were scarcely audible; there was only the rustle of their dresses – the hems of which they held up with their fingertips – as they brushed over the grass.

were, came strolling along quite naked – their hair loose, their firm breasts bobbing, their thighs glowing pink on either side of the black triangle of hair – and occasionally raising their arms to reveal the sweet, dark hollow of their armpits.

The first maiden was walking slightly ahead of the other two, and just then, her voice trembled slightly and faded to a sigh; placing one finger on her lips, she pointed with her other hand. The three stood gazing at the resplendent youth, whose marble skin was gilded with blond hair, like the soft fair hair on his head. And seeing him sigh, they glanced at each other and modestly averted their gaze from such a marvel, in which everything was more and much bigger than any maiden would dare to imagine.

Suddenly the goddesses stopped and stared at him, smiling broadly, eyes aflame, as they took the measure of him from head to toe. A warm tremor ran through him, and a suppressed yearning filled his breast: he sighed.

Their modesty immediately became a fiery fascination. And having first averted their gaze, they now looked around to see

The goddesses smiled at his sigh and drew closer. And their gaze was like an ardent flame licking him all over and to which

if he was alone. Then they went a little closer. His horse, which had been watching them, shook its head and neighed softly.

his pulsating body gradually responded. Tiny cupids fluttered round about, playing flutes.

They trembled and stopped, as if frozen to the spot, afraid he might wake up. He merely breathed more deeply, more intermittently, as if his blood, breathing in tandem, were interrupting that suppressed sigh.

And the goddesses shimmered in the mist now wrapping about them, their eyes urging him not to move. And he merely stretched, revealing still more of his body, and was filled by a sense of overwhelming torpor.

Just then a sudden whirlwind wrapped about him, snorting and snoring. The maidens, wide-eyed, did not dare to understand what was going on, nor would their innocence allow them to. The goddesses, breasts trembling, took turns to hover above him in that whirlwind, and a moist, passionate night closed round him, entombing him. A painful, pleasurable tickle ran through him. The maidens withdrew in terror to the nearby trees, as if a sudden shower of rain had fallen, a rain that drenched the goddesses. And reaching out, hands clasped, he opened his eyes and imagined that the Devil – his endless thirst finally quenched – would now leave him alone for good. He lay there voluptuously for some time, annoyed that the goddesses had disappeared, but feeling, too, a triumphant certainty that he was a man desired by goddesses. He sat up and looked at the quietly flowing water. And, for the first time, he did not want to bathe in the river. On the contrary, he had a feeling of a quiet, delicious exhaustion. He smiled. He stood up. And he studied his own body slowly, calmly, admiringly. He had never before dreamed of goddesses and realised now that he had never hoped so earnestly for another such dream. And the goddesses were just like women. He had a sudden inspiration. He crouched down, put his hat on his head, closed his eyes and made a wish. Would the hat still obey him? He felt a warmth on his lips. A body cleaving to his. Slender hands stroking his back. He opened his eyes. The hat had obeyed. And embracing the three maidens and tearing their dresses, he hurled them to the ground. And they were exactly like the goddesses in his dream. However, panic gripped him and, hurriedly extricating himself from their embraces, he took off his hat. No, that was one thing from which the hat could not save him. And putting the hat back on his head, he commanded that if the maidens were women and not goddesses, it would be as if they had never seen him. And so it was. And while he, invisible, was getting dressed, they sat in a circle on the ground, smoothing their dresses torn by the thorns of the forest, combing their long, wavy hair, and singing this song:

> *To the castle the horseman*
> *Came wending his way,*
> *Knowing not what he sought,*
> *Nor what he would find.*
> *With his lance of gold*
> *He beat on the doors,*
> *For the doors were locked*
> *And the rooms dark and empty,*
> *Apart from a tower,*
> *Where a princess, a prisoner,*
> *With no maid in attendance,*

No maiden, no pomp,
Waited and wept
For who knows who.
The knight beat on the door,
But she did not cry out,
Seeing in his pounding
A promise of freedom,
A breaking down of the door
Her father had intended
To fend off his fear:
Men and their lances.
But this man, with his lance,
Had entered the dark castle
And was climbing the stairs
To find the unknown princess,
Who was waiting above.
The princess stood trembling,
And before she saw him,
She saw his golden lance,
And dazzled by its splendour,
She ran to his arms,
Not knowing the raised lance
Would pierce her through.
Into his arms she fell,
Dying and sighing,
These words she then spoke:
Sir, you come from afar,
Armed with great courage,
To kill me with a death
Of which your love did not know.
And faithful and honest,
I was waiting for you,

For I lived for love
In these darkened rooms.
Her head drooped, and she died,
She would speak no more.
And on the now sullied lance
Her blood glowed red.
Gazing down at the maiden
Lying dead on the floor,
The knight swore that never again
Would he break down castle doors,
So he broke into pieces
His beloved lance
And he buried it deep
Along with the princess
In the grave he dug for both.
And sadly, very sadly,
He went on his way
To the black-walled monastery,
Where he would for ever stay.
But from that grave sprang roses
That withered the hand
Of those who picked them.
Roses of blood and milk
That only the earth would drink.

He had been dressed and ready for ages by the time they had finished singing and had fallen still and silent, as if awaiting an order from him. And he was thinking about the song they had sung: roses of blood and milk that only the earth would drink. Or the Devil. He took off his hat and, holding it in his hand, made a gracious bow. They stood up and very gravely curtsied. They were all propriety and innocence, apart, that is, from the disquieting way in which they kept looking him up and down. A disquiet which they, entranced, made no attempt to conceal, and which filled him with an enjoyable warmth, like a memory retrieved, like a mouthwatering pleasure postponed. One of the maidens was the first to speak:

"Sir, whence do you come and whither are you going? You are not from this place, for we have never seen you at the castle."

"I come from afar and have far to go, but I will go to your castle if your master wishes to receive me like a good host. And I could repay him with my services."

The maiden sighed and said: "Our master is dead. And the mistress of the castle, whom we serve, will not be long in following him to the grave."

At the thought of this great sadness, the maiden's voice broke and she began to sob, and was accompanied in this by the other two maidens. And the horseman asked:

"But is there no hope that your mistress will survive?"

And it was the other two maidens – who were sobbing less bitterly, having only been imitating their companion – who gave their answers, like a priest's practised responses.

"The physicians despair of her life."

"Our chaplain is already praying for her soul."

"But still she waits for a king's son to come."

"Who must embody three very noble qualities."

"He must be very handsome."

The three maidens exchanged glances. And the first one went on:

"He must be a great physician."

Again they exchanged glances. What could the third quality be?

The three blushed and giggled, their heads pressed together.

"What else?" asked the horseman.

One of the other maidens said:

"He must also be…"

And the first maiden completed her sentence: "A virgin."

And their eyes, fixed on him and still brimming with tears, burned like hot coals.

The young horseman smiled faintly and asked:

"Does he really have to be a king's son?"

They again put their heads together and consulted. No, that was not essential. And he said:

"I am the man she is waiting for, then, since I embody all those qualities."

They blushed even more furiously, but, curtseying again, they took him with them to the castle, which appeared at last, at a bend in the river, behind a hill, and was made of very white stone. They went ahead. And following behind, leading his horse, he could not take his eyes off their swaying hips, like hidden moons. Now and then, one of them would turn to him and smile. And it was already dark when they reached the drawbridge.

II

The castle was small, but very ancient; the reason it looked almost newly built was because it had recently undergone extensive renovations ordered by the late husband of the current mistress, when he returned from Constantinople a wealthy man. For he was – or had been – the celebrated Dom Gundisalvo Matamoros of Pendão, who had served the Emperor. The horseman was standing in the *salle d'armes* and was listening to the explanations offered by the castle's plump, waddling chaplain, who had a large head and fat fingers that looked like lard dripping from his black cassock, which, in turn, resembled a wineskin tied in the middle with a belt. In a mellifluous voice in marked contrast to his vast girth, the chaplain, suspicious of the handsome, smiling young man listening to him, then asked whom he served and where he had come from. He asked the same questions over and over in various forms, but the young man always gave the same answer:

"I am the man your mistress is waiting for."

And they were still engaged in this to and fro when one

29

of the maidens came down the stairs – just visible in the all-pervading gloom – which led up to the private rooms above. Having curtsied, she said:

"My mistress asks that the noble physician should come and see her without delay."

However, the young man was in no hurry and first wanted to know what were these deadly ailments afflicting the lady. The priest and the maiden were unable to pinpoint details or causes. The priest believed that her illness dated from the death of Dom Gundisalvo, but the maiden disagreed, saying that the illness was recent and while it had its beginnings in grief, it was not the grief of a widow. The priest said that his mistress neither ate nor drank and was slowly wasting away. The maiden retorted that she ate and drank just as everyone else did or as any lady would who ate well in order to maintain her health; but, in spite of this, she was, nonetheless, wasting away. Both agreed that she sighed a great deal, did not wish to see anyone, spent the days and nights lying in her darkened chamber and no longer had strength enough to get out of bed to attend mass and take the Holy Sacrament. The chaplain held mass in the prayer-room in her chamber, a sacred space with an altar made from a stone that Dom Gundisalvo had taken from the wall of the Holy Sepulchre in Jerusalem and on which stood a holy image of St Recolato of Typhonia, a gift from the Emperor himself. She rarely saw mass through to the end, though, because she sighed and groaned so much that the chaplain had once considered exorcism, and had even consulted the archbishop, a visit that involved a long journey to the city by mule, a true ordeal for a poor priest who could barely walk, let alone ride. When the archbishop learned who he was talking about, he had dismissed him brusquely, saying... Then the maiden said:

"My mistress wishes him to come to her without delay."

She went ahead and, in the gloom, which the torches did little to dispel, her hips appeared to sway still more; with the chaplain behind him, the young man followed the maiden up the stairs and found himself in another grand room. He looked around him, but it did not seem to him to be a bedchamber. There were a lot of people present, all of them young women like the three he had already met, the other two of whom were also present. And the whole assembly were gazing at him yearningly, inquisitively and murmuring appreciative comments.

At the far end of the room, a door he had not previously noticed suddenly opened, and two men advanced towards him; they had pointed beards and wore long black robes as iridescent as a crow's wing. When they entered and went over to the young man, a great silence fell, a silence that became absolute as they stood, in mute hostility, looking him up and down. The young man asked:

"Are you the physicians who have despaired of being able to save your mistress?"

And they replied:

"We are."

"Because we are not the sons of a king. Because we are not handsome. Because our only virginity is our lack of knowledge."

A murmur filled every corner of the room. And then the physicians asked:

"To be the one she says she is waiting for, you must be all those things. Are you?"

"No, I am not the son of a king, but I could be. As for handsome…"

"He certainly is!" chorused the women gathered in the room.

31

"As for the other thing…"

"He is that too," said the maiden, and two more voices seconded hers as she scuttled into the shadows, where the others hurriedly encircled her.

"As for being a great physician, well, we'll see," said the two doctors.

And they immediately began to quiz him. Did he use a baby's navel, boiled or fried? And what about the hangman's rope? How long did he soak it for? And did he do so when the moon was new or on the wane? And what about the dried eye of a black cat? Did he roast it? And the paw of the mole? Did he marinate it in broom or thyme? And other such questions, all intended to demonstrate their great knowledge. Then the young man said:

"But that is witchcraft, not medicine."

A wave of giggling filled the room. And even the priest gave free rein to his laughter, hurriedly crossing himself at the same time.

The two doctors were dumbstruck. And one of them, gaunt and ashen-faced, declared: "The frontier between medicine and witchcraft is that between virtue and faith. In Bologna, in Padua, in Salamanca and in Paris, where I studied, and from where I went on to become doctor to the King of France and the Count of Savoy and the Marquis of Monferrato and the Duke of Lorraine, and the Lord of Biscay, may their souls rest in peace…"

From the room whence they had emerged came a terrifying cry. And the young man said:

"Take me to your mistress before, thanks to you, she joins those illustrious noblemen."

And pushing past the astonished physicians, he walked over to the room and through the door, which he slammed shut behind him. The others were still staring at the slammed door, when it opened again and another lady appeared, saying:

"He sent me away. He wants to be alone with her. But, oh, what a splendid physique, I mean, physician!"

A murmur of approval echoed her words round the room.

… …

Dona Urraca of Biscay, the daughter of Dom Tortozendo Ermiges the Battler, and widow of Dom Gundisalvo Matamoros of Pendão, was lying in her bed. Among the tangle of blankets and furs on the bed, which was wide enough to accommodate at least three couples, he could not make out her body at all. Only her face was visible, eyes closed, her dark hair spread over the white pillows, like a decapitated head, thin and bloodless, left behind at the top of that vast bed. The young man leaned over and observed the long eyelashes, the arc of the eyebrows, the small, sharp nose, the pale, full lips, the very round chin, the colourless cheeks, the shadows under the eyes. Then with one movement, he threw all the bedclothes onto the floor. Lying naked on the white sheet, Dona Urraca did not move or open her eyes. Her skin was the colour of ivory, which, while it stood out against the whiteness of the sheet, at the same time seemed to blend in. Her neck was long and thin, like her bony shoulders. However, below her clavicles lay the curve and counter-curve of her breasts, which, even in that supine position, were still large and firm and crowned by large, dark, taut nipples. Then came her narrow waist, and from her broad hips with their slightly prominent hip-bones rose her rounded belly, which flowed like water into her navel. And her belly, like a furling wave, descended as far as another hillock covered in dense, dark undergrowth before disappearing into the slender valley of her thighs. Her thin arms lay by her sides and ended in hands with long fingers and long nails. Her thighs narrowed down to her sharp knees and thin shins, the calf muscles soft and relaxed. Her ankles looked fragile, though, and only her feet seemed tense, the toes curled and slightly splayed.

The young man studied her minutely, as if this were the first time he had ever seen a naked woman, and it occurred to him that, despite his dream, it was just as if he had never seen one, even though, for reasons he did not understand, he always required the men and women he cured to first show themselves to him naked.

Dona Urraca's legs parted. Waves of heat ran through the young man, and he pictured, inside his own body, the goddesses rolling up into a ball in his belly, and he lent forward, lips parted. When he placed his lips on the acrid smell, he felt hands grab his hair and Dona Urraca's fingers dug into his scalp. However, this lasted only a moment. He had kept hold of his hat all the time, and now he put it on his head and looked up. Moving away from the bed where she still lay motionless, although her eyes were now wide open, he went to the door and called.

The physicians entered the room and, with them, the three maidens, as well as the one he had earlier sent out. He gave his orders. The physicians were to bleed him so that Dona Urraca could take a bath of warm water mingled with his blood. And, for this purpose, he held out his right arm. They were then to take her by the feet and the shoulders and immerse her seven times, head and all, in the water of his chastity. Meanwhile, he would remain lying naked on her bed and would only get up when the seven immersions had taken place. He almost felt tempted to introduce some variation into this his usual remedy. The three maidens who had found him remained there with him until Dona Urraca was brought back from the bath and laid by his side. He smiled to see the look of indignation on the faces of the physicians, on the face of the maiden he had banished from the room and who had immediately covered Dona Urraca up when she returned from her bath, and even on the faces of the three other maidens. And he explained to them that he had certain special powers and was able to make himself invisible. It was then that the chaplain, whom no one had seen come into the room, emerged from the shadows, holding his cross out above his paunch and shouting:

"*Vade retro, vade retro, vade retro, Satana.*"

Everyone recoiled in horror, and Dona Urraca writhed about on the bed, moaning. However, the young man was unimpressed and advanced on the monk, with him taking one step forward and the chaplain one step back, until the latter, making a dull noise like a sack falling to the ground, fell to his knees, wild-eyed and barely able to speak. And it was the young man who helped him up, took him by the arm and led him over to the flickering candles on the altar and made him kneel down, then knelt by his side, blessed him devoutly and intoned the *Salve Regina* in a voice and in a Latin that were both equally marvellous, and with which everyone joined in. Then he got up and said:

"What makes you think that a youth like me, handsome and chaste, who gives his own blood to save the dying, should not also be a good Christian? I have made no pact with Satan. He pursues me just as he pursues you and, while my body is his, my soul belongs to God..."

They all crossed themselves again. The chaplain, however, managed to stammer out a few words, declaring that this was not good doctrine, and that Our Lord God had become flesh through the works and grace of the Holy Spirit, and that the flesh is weak and sinful, easy prey for the Devil, but that God had ransomed that flesh and promised it resurrection. The young man said nothing. He merely began to get undressed and put on his hat. And everything happened as he had said it would.

… …

Lying full-length on the bed, after the blood for the bath had been taken from him and for as long as the bath itself lasted, he felt terribly cold as he always did on these occasions, so cold that he would shiver and his teeth would chatter. And his hands would grip his thighs. This time, however, it was as if a fiery veil had interposed itself between the terrible cold he felt and his inner depths. And his eyes never wearied of looking at the three maidens sitting beside him on the edge of the bed, but who could not see him. Nor would he be visible to the chaplain were he to turn round, although the chaplain was now kneeling, praying, before the altar at the far end of the room. He thought of ordering him to leave, but why, if he could not see him? And so he lay there, waiting and shivering and, despite everything, expecting the Devil to arrive and find him naked and exposed. He did not come. What did come was a desire to reach out his hands to the maidens, who were talking in low voices, although, given the enormous size of the bed, he was unable to hear what they were saying. He felt sure, however, that they were talking about him, and their whispers became part of the protective warmth he felt. He rolled over to the edge of the bed and lay right next to them. And while his hands had fun tickling them and making them jump, he was able to eavesdrop on their conversation.

They were wondering who he was, this extraordinary man,

so young, so handsome, so wise, and who was clearly lying when he said he was not the son of a king. He had doubtless, for vengeful purposes, been stolen at birth and exchanged for another, as often happens with the sons of kings. And one of the maidens, the back of whose neck he was stroking, listed the many well-known or suspected cases, which reminded the others of still more examples, all of which they gravely examined, concluding (when, having slipped his hands under her dress, he was already fondling the breasts of the maiden who had so vehemently reached this conclusion) that it was obvious he was the son of a king. Or, as the third maiden declared – as he was feeling her thighs – the son of a queen, a hypothesis they found seriously seductive. The queen had sinned with a page while the king was away in the Holy Land; and so that he would not discover her adultery, she had given the child to a wetnurse in some distant village; and they had brought the beautiful child to the wetnurse, who had no inkling as to who she was suckling; and then, when the child was older, his godmother, or a lady who said she was his godmother (and who, of course, was his mother in disguise) arrived and took him away; a gentleman was waiting by the roadside, and he took the child with him and taught him the wisdom of this world and the next; and when the gentleman died, the young man sold everything and set off into the world in whose sciences he was already adept, the principal science being that of giving his blood to save the dying.

His caresses helped him gradually to detach himself from the tangled skein in his belly, and from which came an ardour and a certainty that his dreams could have been real, as he lay listening to the three maidens, entranced, because they might actually have been describing his life. It was all true, except that his mother had not sinned with a page, but with a prince who could have been king if two others ahead of him in the line of royal succession had died before him: and his mother had not been a queen or a duchess, but a countess' lady-in-waiting (although the countess had been almost a queen), and the countess would not allow her ladies-in-waiting to marry or to think about men once she had taken them into her affections. There was just one thing the maidens did not know, as they pondered his life, unaware that they knew so much. And he was suddenly filled with a great bitterness, like a wave of cold, the cold he had forgotten: the reason they could so easily imagine his life was that, contrary to what he had always been led to believe, there was nothing unimaginable about it, even though the maidens had begun by thinking there was. Again the warmth started to return to his body and, as it mingled with the icy cold, it filled him with an unbearable longing, such as he had never felt before. No, his life was not like other people's lives, or he was not the same as other people. Who else had a hat like his? Who else had a devil in love with him? Tremors and painful shudders ran through him and lingered here and there in his body. A cold sweat covered him like a damp shroud. Feeling his head vanishing, his limbs separating off from him, as if he were being dismembered, he slithered headfirst down inside the bed. As he did so, he gave a triumphant smile, because this meant the lady was cured. Not, of course, that he had ever doubted she would be, so confident was he of his immense power. He stretched and smiled. He stood up on the bed and amused himself by rubbing his body against the heads of the maidens, who were now still and silent, waiting for their lady to be brought back to them. And then, resting his hands on their heads, he leapfrogged over them onto the flagstones and whirled about the room in a mad dance.

… … … … … … … … … … … … … … … … … … … …

It was night when, in the room filled by the multitude of maidens, despite the best efforts of the chaplain and the physicians to keep them out, Dona Urraca lay next to him, exposed to all eyes, breathing easily, deep in the sleep in which she had recovered her normal temperature. He got dressed then and left the chamber without being seen. In the great empty room beyond, which echoed only with the murmurs coming from the chamber next door, he went over to a window and stood looking out at the dark night. They had completely forgotten about him. He was, after all, a man like any other, who ate and slept and earned his living like everyone else and who had no castle and no trade. Yet he traded in the power he possessed, and should be paid for the blood he gave. His legs and arms felt weak, and a small dark scab had formed on the spot beneath his inner elbow from which they had bled him. He rested his arm on the window sill and studied the now dry wound with some annoyance. How had it all begun? Why did he have to earn his living like this, a wanderer giving his blood, his precious red blood, at once so thick and so liquid, to men and women who were suffering from who knows what? How often had it happened before? Many times. Ever since he had been left alone and set off into the world. Old men and young, married women, spinsters and widows, children and adolescents, had all bathed in his blood in order to recover life and health. And suddenly he wondered: what became of them? Did they live a long time and how had they lived their lives? For he always left shortly afterwards and never saw or heard about any of them again. Suddenly, he remembered that he had not given the necessary advice about what to do with the bath water. He shuddered. That water would cost him his life if he did not get away soon. The guards, the bishop, the theologians, the inquisitors, the physicians, the woman screaming and being blessed, the old lady saying she had seen him cutting up the new-born baby and eating its little hands, and the gallows and the pyre all ready in the main square, and the duke giving the order, and him going up the steps and suddenly, in the midst of it all, becoming invisible at the very moment the executioner placed on his head the hat brought hotfoot by the prison guard to make sure it was burned along with him. Because the water had turned black and fetid, and the judge and the midwife had carried it in jugs to the bishop. He cautiously checked to make sure he was still invisible (which he could do by placing one hand over the other and seeing if he could still see both) and returned to Dona Urraca's chamber, slowly pushing open the door. No one was there. The wax candles on the altar dimly lit the heavy air which smelled, yes, rather like that bath water. He sniffed again and saw the goddesses of his dream lying on top of him. It was a strange smell, but not a bad smell, and it drew him to the bed where Dona Urraca lay sleeping. Again, however, he was beset by those terrible memories, which sent him hurrying across the chamber and through the door into the next room, where the bath had been. In the light from the torches, three heads could be seen emerging from the bath in the middle of the room. He went closer to see who they were, and saw that the heads belonged to the two physicians and the chaplain, who were enjoying a communal sitz-bath.

He could not contain his laughter, which made them leap up, trembling, the two very thin physicians and the chaplain with his plump flesh wobbling. The sight of them made him laugh even more. And terrified and making the sign of the cross, the three men scrambled out of the bath, snatching up the clothes they had left lying on the floor, before fleeing through one of the other doors. He followed them and saw them helter-skeltering down a dark staircase which, to judge by the odour of burning and of food, clearly led to the castle's kitchens. He returned to the bath and leaned over. The water was still and dark, as smooth as glass. However hard he sniffed, he could smell nothing. He observed himself tenderly, pityingly. He was never invisible in mirrors, and in them he looked, he thought, handsome and sad, solitary and somewhat pathetic, with nothing and no one, with only his own image for company. This was why he so enjoyed bathing in rivers, as if plunging into them and splashing about in their waters were a way of bonding with that fascinating image which, unless he himself shattered it, was never invisible and never fully a part of him. What would happen if he ever got into his own bath of blood? He had a vague idea and he shuddered. He would emerge old and shrivelled, blind and deaf, his voice like the cracked voice of a crow. Then he gathered all the saliva he could into his mouth and sent a gob of spit into the water. It began to boil and churn, sending up smoke and clouds of steam, before shrinking back to the bottom of the bath, leaving only a few dried scabs, just like the one on his arm. A small sharp pain ran up his arm and, with some alarm, he saw that the scab had vanished. He again spat into the bath, and this time it was the turn of the dried scabs at the bottom to dissolve into nothing. And the steam hovering in the air descended and condensed into the bath which, little by little, filled up again, this time with pure, limpid, transparent water, in which his image smiled back at him.

He gave a sigh of relief and returned to Dona Urraca's chamber. When he went in, he felt an agitation in the air and saw her, arms outstretched as if blind, scurrying back and forth, gloriously naked, snatching at the emptiness with her long fingers. Holding his breath, he leaned against the wall and waited. She came towards him, as if expecting him to be hanging on the wall like a tapestry. Her hand found his shoulder and she dug in her nails. Then her other arm encircled his head, drawing him down towards her half-open lips bubbling with saliva. Her whole body was pressed violently to his, rubbing against him. And as he felt himself being absorbed by long, deep, intermittent kisses, he heard her saying in a hoarse voice: Yes, yes, I want you like this, invisible. Come.

And still keeping his hat firmly on his head so that it would not fall off, his body now pure, explosive tension, he allowed himself to be undressed by those hands busily exploring every corner of his body, their interrogative fingers leaving not a nook or cranny unscrutinised, while she stooped down and moved around him, kissing him all over; and closing his eyes, he let himself be led over to the bed where – while his body was invisible, the pleasure he was feeling was definitely not – he lost his virginity once and for all.

III

When he awoke, it was as if he had not slept or as if everything had happened during a long sleep in which he had not opened his eyes to see, and during which, precisely because there *was* nothing for his eyes to see, he had nevertheless seen what he could not have seen. A sour taste filled his dry mouth. His arms ached. And his hips swooned, and that swooning feeling reached all the way up to the back of his neck. He stretched and opened his eyes. The first thing he saw was the canopy over the bed. Instinctively, he raised his hand to his head. His hat wasn't there. Frightened, he sat up and looked around him. Dona Urraca had disappeared. He got to his feet, feeling terribly distressed, but then felt so dizzy he immediately sat down again on the edge of the bed. Feeling even more distressed, he again tried to get up, and this time the dizziness had passed. He hurriedly pulled on his clothes, then desperately rummaged about among the bedclothes and in the large wardrobe in one corner of the chamber, everywhere. Then he remembered the small altar flanked by the almost burned-out candles in their tall candlesticks. He opened the altar doors and was just reaching out to pick up his hat, which was lying at the feet of the images within, when he heard someone laugh and he spun round.

Dona Urraca was behind him, and she said:

"Your hat, far more than your blood, was the miracle for which I had so often prayed to the saints. With your hat on, you were invisible. And since you were just as astonishingly beautiful invisible as visible, only you could cure me of my ills. According to what my maidens told me, you were both beautiful and a virgin. You were, they said, a prodigious physician precisely because of your virgin blood, that is what you said and so it proved. But what cured me was being able to love you without seeing you, because you were the same marvellous body I had seen and which is never as marvellous as one imagines it to be. When invisible, you were much more than everything you promised to be when visible. But now you are mine, and I will never weary of you, because – while the gestures of love are always the same, and pleasure can be too if always associated with a particular body – in our case, whenever we wish, whenever we fear that my being able to see you is causing us to grow tired of each other, I can always choose not to see you in order to see you once more in my soul and in the depths of my body which you reach with your body, just as you did when, as my invisible lover, you ceased to be a virgin. Yes, I know you were a virgin, I received undeniable proof of that. For all your knowledge, you could not make your desire and mine coincide. If you were not a virgin, but had never truly felt desire or never desired anything or anyone but yourself, you would have known what to do, as if I were not there. If you were not a virgin, but were experienced in the games of love, and in the pleasure of feeling desired, you would have known what to do as if you gave not a thought to your own desire. And, without me, or so it seemed, you knew neither one thing nor the other."

He listened in amazement and could not stop thinking about his own face reflected in the water and smiling back at him. As if guessing what he was thinking, she went on:

"I also know that you often used to look at yourself, and the only image that smiled at you was your own. But I know, too, that you never assailed your own virginity. Because, if you had, and if you yourself had always been your sole image of love, you would not have given yourself to me as you did, and I would have had a long battle with your image before your desire could acknowledge me; and even when it had, you would have withdrawn from me at once, withdrawing into the embrace of your own image, rather than feel that you had chosen me rather than the space in which that image existed. That did not happen either. When you were looking at yourself, you weren't looking at you, but at what you would be for the person who might one day look at you…"

They were lying together on the bed and she was stroking his hair. She went on:

"Your eyes are asking me how I know all this. And that question asked only by your eyes is further proof, if proof were needed, of your virginity. Because I know all this in a way you cannot possibly imagine. I have slept with countless men, some very young and so inexperienced and frightened that I had to teach them everything, others older and wiser, who I had to humiliate by showing them what they did not know. And I can guarantee you one thing: I came to know what they themselves did not know about themselves. A woman like me knows what men do not know about men. And with you, it was as if everything I know served only to prove your virginity, and as if I had unlearned everything in your arms."

She nestled closer to him, and he felt her other hand pressed against a new desire of which she appeared unaware, and she added: "Because only you truly knew me, and you cannot imagine my amazement on discovering that the emptiness of everything I had previously experienced was even greater than I had imagined. You possessed me in a way no one ever had, in a way I did not even know was possible. I'll go further: I have never experienced with anyone else what I experienced with you. Deep down, I despised those men and their desire, even when I was the one to provoke that desire, or perhaps for that very reason; and now I see that I never gave myself entirely. I felt a kind of horror of them and of myself. But you…" And she gave him a long kiss.

Then, suddenly, he rolled over, covering her body with his, and in repayment for her kisses, he kissed her face, her throat, her breast. And she clutched at his hair and pressed her face to his so that their mouths crushed together. He then pulled away from her and leapt out of bed, but she held on to one of his hands and drew him to her, saying:

"Don't be afraid, because if I could not see you in your invisible state, you did not lose the virginity of your blood. And if you did not lose it this first time, then you never will, and I will be able to see you and be yours. Come here, don't be afraid, don't worry. And in the light of the sun, which is high in the sky now, I will see you as I have never seen any man before."

And when he impetuously gave in, she was the one to get out of bed in order to see him as God had made and placed him in the world, sitting, standing, walking and finally lying on the bed, where she lay down by his side, so that he could disrobe her like her lord and master.

… … … … … … … … … … … … … … … … … … … …

Later, when they were having supper by the window and watching the evening sun gilding the trees on the banks of the river, she leaned across the table and, stroking his face, said:

"I don't even know your name. What is your name, my love?"

"What does my name have to do with anything? What does it matter if my name is this or that? And in truth, I have no name, because the name they gave me is not mine. Besides, I have a different name in every land and every castle that I visit. So, just as you unknowingly deflowered me, leave me nameless. If I am to continue a virgin, even though I no longer am, it's best that I have only the name you give me. And when I leave, you will always remember me by that name, and when I remember you, I will know precisely who I am, having been for you the name that you gave me. What name will you give me?"

"None, because you are speaking to me as if you were sure you would go away, leaving behind a name that no more belongs to you than you belong to those whom you leave with a sweet and beautiful memory. But you are not going to leave. And if, in order for you to stay, you must remain nameless, then I will not give you a name."

"But how can I stay?" he asked, caught between leaving and staying.

She got up and went over to him, for he had remained seated, and leaning against him, stroking his hair, she asked:

"How could you leave? Now, don't tremble like that. I'm not going to hold you here, I'm not going to pursue you, I'm not going to bewitch you. You are entirely free. How could I want to make you a prisoner, even my prisoner, after what you have been to me? If I were to hold you here, even bound with

47

the bonds of a great love that you yourself did not wish to flee, what joy would you feel in my arms and what joy would I feel in yours? You would certainly love me more violently, as if you wanted to kill me with your male weapon, and my pleasure would be redoubled. But afterwards… afterwards, how could I look you in the eye, seeing there a terrible resentment because you were my prisoner, a resentment you would not even admit to yourself, but which I would always see in your eyes, constantly, even when those eyes were burning with desire or when we were engaged in the act of love itself?"

Then he rested his head against her side and stayed like that for a long time, eyes closed, thinking nothing, feeling nothing, only the gently penetrating warmth of purest love. In the sleep that wrapped about him like a glad weariness, his mistress was singing him an old song which, little by little, he stopped hearing, borne away on the current carrying him far from everything and from himself, with a sense that he was not alone on the boat travelling down the river. And certain that he would never ever be alone – anywhere.

> *My sweet friend,*
> *Whom I so loved,*
> *Left one day*
> *Without a word.*
> *And with him took*
> *My one desire,*
> *Leaving me alone,*
> *Alone with this yearning*
> *For my sweet friend.*
> *My sweet friend,*
> *Whom I so loved,*
> *And who never spoke*

When he was with me.
And with him he took
All that I had,
Leaving me alone,
Alone with this yearning
For my sweet friend.

IV

The next day, Dona Urraca decided to go for a walk and visit the place where her maidens had found him. They formed a long, magnificent cavalcade, the preparations for which filled the whole castle with loud voices, the courtyard with clattering hooves, and the rooms and stairs with scampering feet. A joyous wind seemed to blow through everything, sweeping away the shadows, the sombre murmurings, the muffled voices, the people sloping silently off. When the young man, hand in hand with Dona Urraca, slowly descended the main staircase, joyful cries broke out, after an initial astonished silence, punctuated by sharp intakes of breath and open-mouthed amazement. And the same silence surrounded them, when, at the foot of the stairs, they responded to the effusively bowed heads, part of a slow bow intended to measure the couple from head to toe and to delightedly breathe in their perfume.

It was then that he was assailed by a feeling of surprise, which, without really being aware of it, he had already felt on his arrival, which seemed now to be lost in the dark depths of time. Looking all around him, scanning and surveying the

scene, he finally mounted his horse, which neighed out of
sheer contentment, its reins held by one of the three maidens
who had found him. From his horse, while Dona Urraca was
mounting hers, helped by two other maidens, the horseman
examined the vast crowd filling the courtyard. He was the
only man there. They rode through the gate, crossed the
drawbridge, and headed for the river. He and Dona Urraca
went first, and behind – as he saw, because he turned several
times to get a better look – the three maidens were riding along
together, and behind them, a long line of all the other maidens.
It was a magnificent procession, truly magnificent; the lavishly
arraigned horses gleamed in the sunlight, the brightly coloured
dresses glowed, and the veils on the headdresses – some
bicorne, some pointed – fluttered white in the breeze. And he
rode at the head of this cavalcade, the only man.

He turned to Dona Urraca, who was on his left, and his
curious, interrogative eyes met hers, which were smiling, as
were her parted red lips. And in her eyes, he saw that she had
understood the question that was there, evident and obvious.
Dona Urraca held out her hand to him, which he took, and she
held it fast in hers, as if wanting to reassure him and leave all
explanations for later. And he smiled, slightly abashed, and
tried to distract himself by looking back again at the cavalcade.

They were riding along by the river now at the same
leisurely pace. The clear water flickered and flowed, the trees
stirred in a breeze that was also partly caused by their passing,
and the light of the sun, sifting through the leaves or reflected
in fractured form on the surface of the running waters, slid
delicately over clothes, harnesses and faces, all of which
positively breathed youth.

They came then to a clearing by the river, which seemed
to have been scorched by a great fire. Bare, withered trunks

surrounded it, the yellowed grasses were too sparse to cover the burnt-black earth and the few bare rocks, and ahead of them, the waters formed a stagnant, mirror-smooth pool, its surface apparently covered with ashes.

He felt strangely troubled, as if not wanting to recognise the place where he had lain and where the maidens had sung to him; and he could not take his eyes off the waters, which could not possibly have been those of the shallow pool in which he had bathed.

The first maiden, however, came alongside them both, and he heard her say, as she looked straight ahead at the scorched trees:

"This is the place."

He shuddered and looked down at his hands, while a murmur ran through the cavalcade that had come to a halt behind them, and from which he heard only the occasional impatient stamping of hooves. His fine-boned, finely-veined hands were resting on the pommel of the saddle, the reins between his fingers.

"Make everything green again." And when he heard these words, he turned to Dona Urraca in horror.

"There is nothing you cannot do. Make everything green again," she said.

And the maidens all repeated her words: "Make everything green again!", while the three principal maidens surrounded him, with the one who had been at Dona Urraca's side coming round to the front and stopping there so that the neck of her horse crossed over the neck of his horse. And he saw in their eyes the intense light he had seen in the eyes of the goddesses. He stared at Dona Urraca. She was sitting very erect in her saddle, her lips pressed together, a hard, penetrating look in her eyes which seemed intent on commanding both his will and his ability to perform miracles. The other maidens had formed a tight circle about them now, and the two horses, in such close proximity to each other, kept shaking their heads.

Filled with panic, because he had never attempted such a thing, he saw that he had no alternative but to do as asked, and he stood slowly up in his stirrups. The maidens and their horses hurriedly retreated, leaving an empty space around him in which the smell of burning seemed still sharper, more acrid. Even Dona Urraca drew back a little, but her eyes retained that cold, determined, commanding look. Steadying himself in the stirrups, he stood there very erect and, gazing up at the sky, he put his hands to his hat and said softly but firmly:

"Make everything green again."

… … … … … … … … … … … … … … … … … … … …

A great wind got up huge whirling clouds of leaves a glittering explosion of trees rearing horses shrieking maidens whinnying waves a clamour of clothes torn apart by the teeth of the wind bits and bridles glinting horses clapping hands neighing running chased by the wind clothes in shreds drifting on the current like curtains winding about the legs of people and horses huge teeth gripping the gleaming explosion of trunks that whistled as they were lifted into the air galloping moaning hair dishevelled breasts bobbing in the foaming waters tumult of manes and tails hurled against the screams in a flash of greenness, greenest of greens… and the clearing at the river's edge was like a garden of tall flowering grasses of every possible shade of green, and the horses were huddled together in one corner and there before him was Dona Urraca, naked, walking ahead of a vast white and pink and black crowd, all equally naked. He sat back in the saddle, his horse impassive, and looked down at himself. He was the only one who wasn't naked. He gazed around him again. The clearing was not as it had been when he rode down the hill to quench his thirst and bathe in the river. It was now a dazzling spring, so intensely vigorous and brightly coloured that it wounded eyes, arms and legs with a wave of anticipatory pleasure. And he had done all that. Why had it never occurred to him that his hat was omnipotent and not merely an instrument he could use to make himself invisible?

A hand on his knee roused him from this state of enchanted absorption. He was surrounded by women, among them Dona Urraca, who approached, arms aloft, and they were clearly surrounding him in order to lay him low. No, not lay him low exactly, but unhorse him and deliver him over to those hands that would then tear him to pieces. Making his horse rear up, he forged a path through the throng and galloped away. He was pursued by shrill, strident cries, fierce and hoarse, scattered throughout the grove of trees, whose branches whipped against him as he rode. Then, right beside him, someone snickered. And his horse stumbled, threw him off, and was still lying on the ground, legs flailing, when he, shaken and dizzy, managed to raise his head. The cawing, whooping crowd were already nearly upon him. His body ached, and any movement he made was a slow agony. He had just enough time to touch his hat, but they were already a mass of thighs and backs and legs encircling his horse. And although he was sure they could no longer see him and, indeed, were not even interested in him, he fled and hid behind a tree, from where he watched as they tore the horse to pieces and ate its flesh. Dona Urraca emerged from the heaving pile of buttocks, gnawing on a piece of meat dripping blood. Several other women followed suit. And he closed his eyes when the three maidens he knew approached Dona Urraca to bring her a particular body part that made him freeze with horror and he watched as she bit furiously into it, while the rest of the blood-stained crew joined her and the three maidens to form a cheering circle around them.

Those women were witches. He had slept with a witch. They were all witches living in an infernal castle. He had made love to a witch. A witch who loved him tenderly. A witch who ate… And a shudder of fear ran through him and he clutched his hands together just to think of Dona Urraca's half-open mouth and her white teeth. And he commanded that everything should go back to the moment when he had made the clearing green again.

… … … … … … … … … … … … … … … … … … … …

There was no sign of his horse or of the women. Oblique, parallel bars of light were pouring tranquilly in through the branches of the trees. A squirrel jumped down and went over to where the banquet had been, and there it sat and slowly ate, its tiny fingers shelling a fallen fruit. And the faintly noisy silence was simply that of a wood in the morning, with no people and no horses.

He emerged from behind the tree and went towards the squirrel. The squirrel did not see him, but felt him and, in two short leaps, had jumped out of his way. He walked very cautiously, listening intently, then he heard someone walking by his side. He stopped. And again he heard that snicker. He asked angrily:

"Why did you make my horse stumble? Why did you burn the clearing? Just for it all to end in that horror?"

And he sat down on the ground and wept: "A witch, a witch, a witch…"

In his ear, the familiar voice, which he had not heard for a long time, whispered: "You're the one who's a witch. You've already been tried and condemned for precisely that crime. And you escaped thanks to witchcraft. Don't you remember?"

He lay flat on the ground, weeping desperate tears and pounding the earth with his fists. Yes, he was a witch, which is why witches loved him.

And the voice murmured: "You're such a child. They love and desire you as women. And it was because she had made a man of you that she wanted to devour you... And for them, your horse was you, given the hunger and thirst for love that consumes all the women who live in that castle. For there have been no men in the castle since Dona Urraca was widowed, except those who happened to pass by and were unaware of the dangers of accepting her hospitality. They were all killed just as they killed your horse. No man lasted more than a night."

He propped himself up on one elbow and asked: "And will I last only a night?"

For answer there was only the silence, and so he answered himself: "No, I lasted two nights and a day... I am not like other men."

And after wiping away his tears and brushing himself down, he followed the sound of sweet feminine laughter and voices. He paused nervously on the edge of the clearing. But everything was as it had been on the afternoon when he first arrived there: no scorched trees, no verdant spring. The maidens were sitting on the river bank, next to Dona Urraca. He heard a soft neighing. And looking round, he saw his horse grazing nearby, along with the other horses, and saw it shake its mane and tail to show its pleasure at his return.

There was a flutter of headdresses and veils too as soon as he entered the clearing, and Dona Urraca waved to him affectionately.

He stopped near her, inside the circle of maidens, and frowning, he asked:

"Where are all the men?"

"What men?" asked Dona Urraca, and an anxious murmur ran around the circle.

"Why are there no men at the castle? Why are there only women? Where are the men?"

"The men... What men? Why do you want to know?"

"Because I do."

"But there's nothing to know."

"What do you mean 'there's nothing to know'? Where are the men who stayed at the castle and were eaten?"

He froze at the sound of muffled screams and scampering feet, but the women had merely run in horror to the far end of the clearing, covering their faces with their hands. Dona Urraca stood up and fixed her eyes on his.

"Is that what you think of me?"

"I just want to know."

"Know what?"

"Everything. I want to know."

Her face crumpled into lines he had never noticed when he had touched her in order to know her with his hands and eyes. Her eyes grew dull with tears. She bowed her head.

"You really want to know."

"I do."

"And if..."

"No. I promise... Oh, my love!" and he embraced her passionately, kissing her and pressing her face to his. She did not respond, but continued to weep. And he embraced and kissed her still more frenetically, while her silent weeping found a chorus in her maidens' moans. They remained like that for a long time, until Dona Urraca gently pushed him away and looked at him, saying:

"I can deny you nothing. It will be as you wish. Come with me."

And she galloped back to the castle, with him at her heels.

V

As they approached the castle, instead of entering via the drawbridge, Dona Urraca took a path that skirted the walls. Behind the castle, an area he had never visited, was a long, broad ditch, and there they stopped. Scrawny, yellow dogs were wandering about, scratching around among the detritus and rubbish from which rose a tenuous mist, giving off a sickly, suffocating smell. It was the castle's dungheap, but so vast you would think the castle was a gigantic barracks, not a private home.

The smell made him dizzy and clung to clothes, face and hands. It was so strong and so tenaciously viscous that his horse kept snorting and anxiously pawing the edge of the ditch.

"They're here," said Dona Urraca in a faint voice that was in marked contrast to the determined way in which she was staring down into the ditch. "There are a lot of them."

He gazed at the ditch for a long time, uncomprehending or unwilling to comprehend, and he only really came to his senses again when, far now from the smell that still clung to his nostrils and to everything, he found himself and his horse riding almost alongside Dona Urraca, who was trotting back to the main entrance to the castle. They rode across the drawbridge, and Dona Urraca dismounted in the empty courtyard, at the foot of the steps.

He remained mounted, and she looked up at him.

"Come. I want to tell you everything first."

He dismounted too and went up the stairs just behind her and, as if carried along by the rustling breeze from her dress, followed her to her chamber.

Dona Urraca stood with her back to him in the bay of the large window and began to speak. But what he heard inside him was quite different.

I was very young and very innocent when my father married me to Gundisalvo. We did not live here then, but at the Emperor's court or in the encampments in Asia, in the service of the Emperor's army. Gundisalvo was much older than me and had been widowed three times before marrying me. It was said that he had killed his other wives, as my maidens and my nursemaid all warned me. I was so terrified that I spoke to my father about it. I can still see him roaring with laughter, saying that Gundisalvo was his brother in arms, and that maidens and old maids knew nothing about men, nor what married women could

I was very young, but I had dreamed of men day and night ever since I saw my father naked. When my father told me that he wished to see me married to Gundisalvo, who was his brother in arms and very like him in manners and behaviour, I dreamed only of Gundisalvo and his sword – which hung from his waist – entering me and tearing me, as I dared not dream that my father would do, and as I had seen him about to do to a maiden who was screaming. And when I was told that Gundisalvo's three wives had died, I was very afraid, but I thought that to be a real wife and my father's wife, it was necessary to die like that. I die of. I was trembling with fear. And I told him, if that were the case, and I had to go and live far from him, then I did not wish to marry. I also said that I could not understand how he could marry me off to someone so much older than me, someone who had already had time to kill off three wives. Did he want him to kill me too? My father stopped laughing and very affectionately sat me on his knees. Stroking my hair, he explained that Gundisalvo was not old, just as he was not old, and I only thought they were old because young women always think their fathers are old. And that he had known Gundisalvo's three wives: one had died in childbirth (and I swore to myself that I would never have children), another had deflowered a page and Gundisalvo had ordered both to be killed, she by having her head cut off, and the page by having everything plus his head cut off (and I swore that I would never have any pages in my service), and the third died of a disease of the internal organs, because she was not perfect and was therefore of no use to Gundisalvo (and I swore that, if my father thought me perfect,

was afraid of something else too, and that fear made me tremble. I would belong to Gundisalvo, and he would take me far away and would kill me, without my father there to sit me on his knee, which was my greatest pleasure. If Gundisalvo's three wives had not survived, it was because he had not been a brother in arms to their fathers. But my father explained how they had died. One in childbirth (and I swore that I would only have children that were not Gundisalvo's), another because she had been unfaithful to him with a page who was still a virgin (and I, like all other high-born girls, ordered any pages to show me what they had, but they were never like my father, and I swore that I would only have at my service full-grown men, so that I could see if they were or were not the same as him and Gundisalvo), and the third because she was not right for Gundisalvo (and if I was not right either, I would die as contentedly as I hoped to die). As soon as we were married, on the very day of the wedding, Gundisalvo carried me far away, at the head of his army, to take charge of a far-flung frontier at then Gundisalvo would feel the same). As soon as we married, I saw that Gundisalvo was not at all as my father judged him to be, and I wept bitter tears. And how could I open my heart to my father and run home to him when my husband had accepted the governorship of a distant region? And, besides, soon after that, my father died in a battle with the Arabs. I could not understand how the two wives Gundisalvo had not killed could have died of what it was said they had died of. But I could understand about the one who had been unfaithful to him, doing with a page what he did not do with me and what he had probably not done with her. Gundisalvo left me alone for long periods and, when he returned, he was like a kind father to me. At night, lying in his arms, as he wanted me to before sleeping, I often tried to make him not a father, but the husband blessed by the Holy Mother Church, the husband who was my right, and to whom my father had given me. Until one day, when he was more than usually tender towards me, I asked what he had done with his other wives and if, like me, he did not want to have

the request of the governor. And the first night we pitched camp, I saw that he and his horsemen were very different from how I imagined men could be. They were like two pages I once came upon unexpectedly. And standing in their midst, Gundisalvo was laughing and saying that my father was his brother, which is why he had kept me for him until I was old enough to marry. And that he would be a father to me. And they all roared with laughter, frolicking and rolling about in front of me, lifting up their tunics. The more I screamed and covered my eyes with my hands, the wilder they became, and it was then that Gundisalvo called one of them over and ordered him to deflower me with the hilt of his sword, and while the others held me down, he did just that. Only you, of all the men I have known since, could make me forget that night. When Gundisalvo went off to war for months at a time, I was left alone in the castle, a dark, gloomy castle, lost among a grim, murky marshland, and guarded by women who dressed like men and slept with each other, and who made me sleep with them.

children. And he told me that, when my father died, everything had died for him, but that he would look after me as if I were his daughter. If I was unhappy, though, he would go away for ever, and I would be free to live as I chose and find a different kind of man. I said nothing and lay there, dry-eyed. That same night, he left never to return. Alone in my room, knowing that he would not come back, I felt quite desperate. I summoned one of his squires, who was a pleasant fellow, and ordered him to have his way with me. He was terribly afraid, but he made a woman of me. Afterwards, whenever he was in the castle, I would find an excuse to be alone with him. And our feeling of fear and respect for Gundisalvo only redoubled our pleasure.

When Gundisalvo returned from his forays into enemy territory, he would sleep with me, and one of his men would sleep with us too, sometimes more than one. But none of them – and they were handsome men – slept on my side of the bed. However, there came an evening when one of them, passing me in a corridor, seemed to hesitate, and so I turned, grabbed hold of him and dragged him off with me to my room, and made of him the man he was not, and I could finally have the man I had not had. After that, whenever he came to bed with us, we would wait until Gundisalvo was asleep... And that made my chosen lover even more ardent.

He waited for her to go on, for, as dusk invaded the room, she had fallen silent. However, when she remained standing with her back to him and still did not speak, he got up from the stool on which he had sat to listen, went over and put his arms around her. She leaned back against him, her head on his shoulder. Only then, eyes closed, did she speak again, and this time he heard her voice alone:

"Gundisalvo left with his soldiers, and I knew he would not come back. But his squire kept making demands, wanting to be paid and threatening to run away to his master and tell him I had seduced him. I had to kill him myself, alleging that he had assaulted me in my room. I travelled from castle to castle, from town to town, through forests, over mountains, down rivers, never looking at a single man, until I came to this castle, which belonged to me and was far from everything. It actually belonged to Gundisalvo, and since I wanted to erase everything that reminded me of the past, I made many changes to the castle, and it was here that I received news of my husband's death and of the riches which, in accordance with his last will and testament, were being sent to me from Constantinople, where he had died in the service of the Emperor, who greatly admired him. Those riches allowed me to create the household I wanted. Only young women would serve me, no men. And any men who happened by would sleep with me and with whichever maidens wanted to sleep with them, until the men died of exhaustion. Gradually, though, rumours about this castle began to spread, and the legend grew up of a castle inhabited only by women, all waiting for men to devour. I don't know how the legend spread, but travellers became few and far between. And I was also waiting and hoping for one man to arrive who would be a virgin in body and soul, which travellers never are. Only he could restore to me the life I had lost even before I had it. With those men I learned that one can only find satisfaction in the satisfaction of one's beloved. And I did not and could not love any of them. But you were different, and you were the man I was waiting for. When my maidens first came upon you, they saw in you a man the mere sight of whom was satisfaction enough. And that is what saved you and what saved me. Because, as time passed, I was gradually fading away. Latterly, I wasn't even interested in the men they brought to me. I would lie on my bed, dying little by little, for I wanted only to die, and hearing the maidens with those men for whom they felt no spark of love, made me want to die all the sooner. My maidens feared my imminent death and summoned physicians and a chaplain. Not the ones you saw, but different ones. I lost count of the physicians who came and gave up, of the chaplains who heard my confession and refused to believe me. I know this whole story is quite simply incredible. But I am sure that you, whose powers are limitless, will believe me, now that you have known me, and now that you know the man you are."

In the long silence that followed, he asked:

"Where are the physicians? And the chaplains?"

She shuddered and said: "What do you mean 'where are they'?"

"I haven't seen them since the night of your bath, when I found all three of them in the tub and saw them flee down the kitchen stairs."

"They were in my bath?"

"They were."

"Doubtless in order to reinvigorate their old age by bathing in your chaste blood," and she laughed out loud and turned to kiss him.

But he stopped her: "Where could they have gone? What if they've gone to complain to the archbishop? What if they tell him everything?"

"Why would they do that if they were reinvigorated and had recovered their youthful virility? They'll be somewhere around in the castle."

"And what if that isn't what happened?"

"How could it not? What else could have happened to them after sitting in a bath that gave me your love?"

"They were perhaps left all shrivelled and withered, even more shrivelled and withered than they were."

The relief she had felt at having confessed to him, the relief that had made her a carefree maiden again, suddenly vanished as his fears struck home.

She summoned her maidens. And together they scoured the castle from top to bottom, from end to end, even the subterranean dungeons and the dovecotes in the towers, but in vain.

… … … … … … … … … … … … … … … … … … … …

They passed a very troubled night. The maidens continued their search of the castle. And despite the love that filled him and Dona Urraca, and which they ceaselessly expressed as they lay side by side in bed, even they could not find, in a moment of satiety, sufficient peace or repose to fall asleep folded in each other's arms.

In the morning, a group of maidens burst into the room in tears, demanding that he, with his magic powers, must save them. Sitting on the bed, and covering his nakedness with the sheet, he looked back and forth between the maidens and Dona Urraca, who remained lying down. And strangely enough, his state of perplexity was only increased by the sight of the principal maiden's breasts, for, in her affliction, her breasts seemed about to leap out of her dress, breasts as firm as those of Dona Urraca.

But what could he do? And he could think of nothing else but those breasts. He only vaguely heard the shouting that ensued when he reached out to touch one of those breasts, uncover it fully and squeeze it.

It was as if this were the signal they had been waiting for. The maiden leapt on him, and he only just had enough time to put on his hat and make himself invisible. Besieged as he was, however, this did not help at all, because some of the maidens grabbed hold of him, even in his invisible state, while others took turns to mount him. And he would certainly have died or been torn to pieces had he not managed to hang on to his hat and resolve to satisfy them all.

When it was over, the scene resembled a cemetery of maidens, for they were everywhere, on the bed, on the floor, some on top of each other, in a tangle of legs and arms and breasts and dishevelled heads, all serenely sleeping.

And only then did he see Dona Urraca standing beside the bed as she had been all the time. Terrified, and without taking off his hat, he looked up at her. Her calm, smiling face gazed down at him as if she could see him; and in a gentle, affectionate voice, she murmured:

"There's no need now for you to remain invisible..."

He still did not take off his hat, and said nothing.

"You can reappear now. Don't hide away like a child who's been naughty and is sure his mother will beat him when he comes out of his hiding place."

But he refused to take off his hat and, getting up very slowly, he went over to her and suddenly pushed her onto the bed. Dona Urraca laughed. And the game ended with the maidens dancing around them, clapping and singing:

> *Dona Urraca's physician*
> *Can cure all ills.*
> *When Dona Urraca moans,*
> *What need for pills?*

Generous to a fault
To each and every maid,
If one should catch a chill
She sends this physician to her aid

Dona Urraca's physician
Can cure all ills.
When Dona Urraca moans,
What need for pills?

No one sees that he's naked.
When his hat's on his head,
And the potion he offers?
Raw flesh – so it's said.

Dona Urraca's physician
Can cure all ills.
When Dona Urraca moans,
What need for pills?

He can cure all diseases,
This prodigious physician,
But what he's best at is treating
A maiden's condition.

Dona Urraca's physician
Can cure all ills.
When Dona Urraca moans,
What need for pills?

Dona Urraca had known only
The griefs of a wife
Until he appeared
And put an end to such strife.

Dona Urraca's physician...

Sitting up and smoothing her dress, Dona Urraca silenced them with a gesture and said:

"Now I am proud to say that you have all experienced the same happiness as I have. And because, like a truly free man, he was bold and brave enough to want you to do just that, I love him all the more, were such a thing possible. I would not want to keep to myself the man who saved me, without you all knowing my good fortune. But now that you have known him as I knew him and can see with your own eyes how fortunate I am, without so much as his shadow touching me, enough is enough."

Still invisible, and leaning on one elbow, he was watching the scene with great amusement. And the first damsel said:

"Let him bring the dead men back to life and let them love us as he loves you, my lady."

"Certainly not," he said, and he said this so vehemently that he suddenly became visible again.

With a thunderous clamour, the women all shouted "Yes! Yes!"

And Dona Urraca considered the proposition. "If the physicians and the chaplain have fled in order to accuse us, then it would be better to bring the men back to life. That way we would have an army to defend us."

"An army?" he asked.

The maidens (?), counting on their fingers, consulted among themselves and with Dona Urraca. The knight from Armenia had been the first. The Lord of La Marche. The troubadour Peter from Cornwall. The other troubadour called Tebaldo. The two brothers from France. Prince Turidante. Alfonso González from Asturias. Nepolemo from Tripoli. The one who called himself the Duke of Brittany. The Count of Béarn. The knight Estêvão de Giscar. The Paduan merchant. The band of thieves led by Charles de Lorraine. Charles de Lorraine himself. The Lord of Trebizond... This listing of names, once they had eliminated any repeats, went on for hours. And then there were the servants, squires, pages, musicians and jugglers who travelled with those people. Dona Urraca did a very careful recount, then turned to him and said: "Yes, an army. There are over five hundred of them."

He sat down on the bed, hugging his knees. "But isn't that too many people? Where are we going to put them all? And who will be in charge of them? Who could possibly impose order on that Babel of men?"

Dona Urraca tapped him playfully on his hat: "This."

"And what if my hat gets worn out? Because I have never done so many things, performed so many great feats, in such a short space of time."

An apprehensive murmur ran through the assembled crowd. And he began pacing back and forth before them, pondering what to do. Then he reached a decision and gave his instructions.

"Each of you will suck a little blood from my veins. It is no longer chaste or virginal blood, but we no longer need it to restore health to anyone, but to instil obedient love into a mob of resuscitated men. Then you will go to the burial ditch and

70

spit out the blood. Each maiden will, I believe, be able to claim rights over those who lie beneath the place where she spits. I will then give an order and will stand by the ditch with my hat on and say: 'Gentlemen, rise up and rejoice and sing the praises of your liberator.'"

And so it was. The ditch began to seethe with such activity that the yellow dogs fled, and grasping hands emerged, along with earth-smeared heads, shoulders, arms and torsos. And while some were almost free already, others were still reaching up with their hands amidst a great clamour of voices. Dona Urraca stood by his side, along with the maidens (?) who watched wide-eyed and open-mouthed. Only he seemed to see nothing, gazing up at the sky, his arms reaching out over the ditch.

And at the bottom of the ditch, which had grown still deeper, the multitude cried out:

"Where is the right hand of he who speaks? And where are all our hard-won privileges? Come quickly and give us the privileges we once lost."

And they looked up, too dazzled by the light to be able to see him standing commandingly above them.

"There you have the privileges that every man most longs to savour in peace. Let each man follow his lady and obey her in everything, and from her he will receive all the prizes he lost."

The multitude swarmed out of the ditch and ran after the maidens, who, at first, recoiled at this surge of humanity. Then they ran, shouting and screaming and dragging the men after them to the castle.

He remained motionless and absorbed, standing by the edge of the ditch, which smelled now of strange perfumes. And he only revived when Dona Urraca knelt down and embraced his legs, weeping and saying: "You're a god, you're a god, you're a god."

Bending down to help her up, a question flashed through his mind: "Was he a god?"

VI

In the castle, the days passed gaily. There were games, banquets, walks, hunting expeditions with those five hundred or so men, who had quite forgotten their position in society, and were made equal in sharing the same pleasures and submitting to the same rules of obedience, enjoying their ladies with not a flicker of jealousy, even though there were about ten men to one lady. He presided over all this alongside Dona Urraca, and was worshipped like a god. And the multitude of men and women never wearied of seeing him appear and disappear in her arms, something which was greeted with wild acclamation.

It was then that he began to feel a kind of yearning, which left him standing for hours at the windows of their room, not sure if the cold he could feel was inside him or if it signalled the arrival of winter. He would stand there, watching the sky change colour, which depended on the clouds, the height of the sun, or on whether the sun was setting. He watched the blue, orange, green, pink, white or grey, and how these changed as they mingled or succeeded each other in bands of colour that emerged then faded, watching until his eyes ached or until the cold drove him inside. He watched the rain too, which was frequent now, and fell in torrents or in thick threads or rhythmic drops or as a fine dust that danced in the air.

Dona Urraca came to stand silently by his side, waiting for him to wake from his melancholy, for only she could rouse him from his contemplations. He would embrace her then, overcome by a sudden, desperate wave of desire, from which he would emerge sadder still. And during the night, whether it was dark or lit by icy moonlight or by the stars glittering in the black sky, there he would be again, staring out into space, filled with a nameless sadness.

At night, too, Dona Urraca would wait for the sudden movement that would drive him into her arms, but though the same passion bound them together, the melancholy never left him.

Dona Urraca said nothing to him, living the festive life of the castle by his side, when, that is, he chose to take part – and, when he did, he was like a madman unchained, and the others would follow his example, infected by his frenetic energy – and she said nothing when he left the others and went up to his room, where he would again stand staring out of the window.

One day, when she had perhaps waited longer than usual for him to come to her, Dona Urraca heard him talking softly to himself, which he had never done before. She listened hard, but he fell silent.

When she went over to him the next day, at the same hour and in the same place, he said, without turning round:

"You know, I…"

"You can leave whenever you want to. Do you remember what I told you? My love for you is too great for me to hold you here. Go. You know that I will wait for you."

"No, it isn't that. You also said I was a god. And I feel that

I am. Or I feel that I am being a god. And it's just unbearable."

She drew back, eyes wide, and covered her face with her hands, but she said nothing. He went on:

"It's unbearable. It's like being on the edge of an abyss and feeling dizzy, and leaning further and further over and feeling afraid of falling and falling and never reaching the bottom, because there is none. And when you're falling like that, you wish there were. The sky is made up of many skies until the last sky. The earth has many layers and one final layer. The sea has a lot of water until it meets the next layer of earth. It's the same with life, everything I have had and that you have given me. Or power, because I can, if I want, have all the power in the world. But all those things have an end, and they will end somehow. Only this abyss has no end, no bottom. And every day I feel worse, or perhaps better, I'm not sure."

He turned to her and saw how sad his words had made her. He embraced her tenderly. And Dona Urraca said:

"I don't know how I can help you, my love. For better or worse, I am now nothing to you and can do nothing for you. Why don't you set off into the world again? Would you like me to go with you?"

"But I don't want to leave, no, I don't even want that."

"What do you want, then?"

"I want to die."

Dona Urraca smothered a scream and recoiled.

"Don't say that, don't, your wish might be granted."

"So be it."

Dona Urraca grabbed him by the shoulders and her nails dug into his flesh: "No, if you want to stop being a god, there's no need to die. You have only to go back to being a man, the man you were, virgin and pure, before you met me. And for nothing of what happened to have happened. Ask to go back to the moment before my maidens saw you. Ask for them never to find you. No, don't ask, command it. Yes, I want you to command it."

He looked at her for a long time and saw in her hard, determined eyes the pain of not having known him and the great love that wanted him to live. And closing his eyes, he made his wish.

… … … … … … … … … … … … … … … … … … … …

Carefully setting his hat down beside him, he drank long and gratefully. The water was very cold, much colder than you might expect in the height of summer there in the valley, so cold that a shiver ran through him. The water was so clear, though, that he would, he decided, take a quick bath, merely to wash and refresh himself. And seated on the ground, he began to take off his boots. The horse had moved away in search of lusher grass. Barefoot now, he slowly rubbed his feet, childishly wiggling his toes as if he were about to count them. Then he got up, unbuckled the broad gold-studded belt and put it down beside the boots and the hat. His long tunic hung loosely about him. Bending down, he grasped the edges of the tunic and drew it up over his head. His long, fair hair, sticky with sweat, fell in soft disorder, and he ran his fingers through it to untangle it. Before undoing the lace tie holding up his brief undergarment, he again looked about him. Not a sign of anyone. He stood there completely naked. And just before entering the water, he ran his hands over his body as if defiantly exhibiting himself. He heard a familiar mocking laugh. And arching his eyebrows expectantly, an expectation he had never before felt, he went back and lay languidly down on the fine grass. Long caresses ran lightly over his skin, whispered kisses nipped his body all over, hands lingered on his crotch, a hardness pressed against him... With a voluptuous moan, he embraced the empty air, rolled over and surrendered to the Devil, who did with him as he wished, and to whom he did whatever he desired; and he lay panting, unsated by pleasures he had never before felt. When it was over, he got up, brushed himself off, ran his hands over his now grubby body, and took a voluptuous pleasure in being grubby. He put on his tunic, glanced dismissively at the river, and went back to his horse. He jumped on and trotted along the river bank. At a bend in the river, behind a hill, he saw a castle made of very white stone. What castle could it be? But the castle was still far away, his horse was weary, and it was growing dark when he reached the open drawbridge. The horse's hooves drummed on the wooden boards. He went in through the gate. In the courtyard, which he vaguely recognised, probably because it resembled that of other similar castles, there was not a soul to be seen. He dismounted and tethered his horse to a metal ring next to the large staircase. He went slowly up the stairs, expecting someone to appear. But the *salle d'armes* was also empty. The sound of his boots echoed around him as he walked purposefully over to a door at the far end of the room. He pushed the door open. Inside was a dark room, with a vast bed in it. He went closer until he could vaguely make out a body lying on it. Only the face was visible, eyes closed, dark hair spread over the white pillows, like a decapitated head, thin and bloodless, left behind at the top of that vast bed. He leaned over and observed the long eyelashes, the arc of the eyebrows, the small, sharp nose, the pale, full lips, the very round chin, the colourless cheeks, the shadows under the eyes. He leaned closer still, the eyes in the head opened and...

… … … … … … … … … … … … … … … … … … … …

her hard, determined eyes, as hard as the nails he could feel digging into his shoulders, were still staring at him with the pain of never having known him and with the great love that wanted him to live, even if she had never known him.

He pulled free of her and sat down on the floor, sobbing: "Why? When you try to go back, it never works. Never. I'm too soiled and grubby now to be yours any more."

She bent down and stroked him, as if she were consoling a child, and said:

"There is nothing that my love for you cannot wash away."

He shook her off, like a hurt child: "No, you don't have the power to do that."

"Why not? Do you think I don't know what happened to you?"

He looked at her in horror, a horror that made him spring to his feet.

"You know about *him*?"

"Why wouldn't I? He was always with us in bed. As soon as you got undressed, he would be there lying beside you. How could I love you the way I do and not feel him close at hand like a poor, unhappy rival? He's here right now, but he doesn't dare show himself. From the moment when you, all unknowing, set off to find me, he knew that he would never have what he has still never had. That's not because of me or your powers. It's because in my arms you became the love of which he knows nothing, the pleasure he cannot feel, and the furious joy that, even without love, does not exist in the lewd pleasures he can offer."

They embraced. And she went on: "Do you know something? I felt sorry for him. He must know how happy you make me. He won't want to lose you as you are now, this marvel, this delight that makes my whole life golden, as if life were the same colour as your hair. And, if necessary, he will protect you rather than taking advantage of you."

He whispered in her ear: "And how do you know and think all this? Simply because you love me? Or because you are he?"

And she replied in a hesitant voice: "Do you still want to die?"

He did not have time to answer, because at that point, they heard the clamour, the tumult, the clank of weapons, the bellowing voices, and then the door being flung wide, letting in a torrent of legs and spears, in the midst of which the roly-poly chaplain emerged from a litter and stood there, shrieking in a high falsetto voice:

"There they are! Seize them! And whatever you do, don't let him put on that hat!"

VII

The trial lasted years, with everyone being examined: the principal accused, the secondary accused, the accomplices, the bewitched who were, therefore, only indirectly responsible, the witnesses, the deponents, the experts, the theologians. Then came the cross-examination of the principal accused, the secondary accused, the accomplices, the bewitched who were, therefore, only indirectly responsible, the witnesses, the deponents, the experts, the theologians (including, among these, reports on the entrails of all the animals found in the castle). Then, because those two initial stages were intended only to verify facts and responsibilities, in order to separate out those implicated into distinct groups, for they would all be tried differently, the whole process began again so as to determine the precise extent of each individual's guilt, and the relative importance of the confessions, evidence, declarations, expert statements and relevant theological and canonical points. It was then that the Holy Office of the Inquisition discovered, purely by chance, that what appeared to be a simple case of witchcraft and a pact with the Devil, involving collective bedevilments unlikely to spread to the rest of the world, was, in fact, a gigantic conspiracy by the Devil against the established order, and involved murders, vampirism, sodomy, a whole range of crimes against nature, and a vast web of subversive propaganda, which included such crimes as curing illnesses, resuscitating the dead and travelling back in time. The trial began again, according to the rules applicable in cases of high treason, atheism, sacrilege, sedition, incitement to disorder and heresy. Then it was adjourned, because it was deemed necessary to conduct a careful investigation into the lives and actions of numerous mostly high-ranking people dead and disappeared, whose lives and actions can only be probed with infinite caution, and, as with State secrets, at the risk of turning the inquiry into an instrument of subversion rather than one intended to maintain order. When the Holy Office of the Inquisition was satisfied that it had mastered all the past facts (and the discovery of a previous trial was a decisive factor), the trial was reopened – on a new basis. This meant re-interrogating the principal accused, the secondary accused, the accomplices, the witnesses, the deponents, the experts, and even once again the theologians and the specialists in canon law. The court then ran up against the inevitable difficulties it always faced, especially after a long adjournment. Many of those involved had died in the meantime, including some who had been resuscitated and were important witnesses for the prosecution. The trial was then divided up into several trials, a sensible way, in the whole court process, of breaking down the gigantic conspiracy which, if judged in a single trial, would have a disproportionate impact on the secrecy essential in such delicate crimes. Once this breaking-down process had been completed – and which necessarily involved reformulation and reclassification, so that one person did not appear in two separate indictments – various partial trials were set up. And only then, as is only logical, could it be said that the trials proper had begun.

Many years passed before that final phase was reached. Periodically, the members of the court would go together to visit the lead criminal in his dungeon, in order to see clear proof of his diabolical nature, namely, that despite the passing years, during which he had remained incommunicado in a subterranean cell without fresh air or daylight, with not even a drain as a channel of communication with the outside world, only the barred door, through which he was kept under constant watch, chained by stout chains to the wall (one round his neck, another round his waist and one on each leg and arm), as well as a special iron chastity belt, and with food reduced to a minimum, none of this had aged him or diminished by one iota his youthful radiance or fearsome beauty. He did show all the external signs of deep repentance and was almost always to be found sitting in one corner, hunched forward with his head on his knees. He did not even look up when the light from the torches made his fair hair gleam. He had to be ordered to get up, and the guards had to drag him to his feet. Then he would stand, leaning against the wall, his body covered in grime, his feet resting humbly on the dried crust of the stinking dejecta in which he had to lie or sit. Despite all this, the members of the court could see, collectively and personally, that his beauty and youth remained unalterably the same. With the passing of the years, those same members of the court, who were, naturally, old men broken by study and fasting and by sleepless nights devoted to eradicating diabolical errors, were not the same at all. The visit was still valid, though, in that there were always a few left who had participated in the previous visit.

Not only his beauty and youth survived. There was

something else too. While he always cooperated in the interrogations and never denied the evidence of his crimes, even though the questions were always indirect, intended to confirm the court's convictions and proofs, and even though he had not yet been informed of the grave accusations hanging over him, the truth is that his humility and his evident repentance concealed a quite different purpose: to resist by dint of submission.

The court considered then how to break down both the resistance of that purpose and the purpose of that resistance. Five men were involved in these deliberations, presided over by the chief inquisitor, who, given the scale and extent of the crimes over time and space had been especially appointed by Rome. He was Brother Anthony of Salzburg, bishop *in partibus* of Heliopolis, and a famous expert and writer of treatises on matters infernal. The other four, who contrasted sharply with the diminutive stature of that great man, were Brother Athangild of Canterbury, "hammer of heretics", Brother Demetrios of Syracuse, "enemy of alchemy", Brother Bernard of Saxony, "visited by the Virgin" and Brother Bermudo of Villaruanda, "sluicer-out of sodomy".

Brother Bermudo was the first to speak, pointing out that the articles in the Regulations had not been applied in strict order and wondering if the trial might, therefore, have certain procedural deficiencies. He concluded by saying: "I must confess to your Reverences that I am somewhat perplexed about one canonically decisive point, which has not as yet been remarked upon: why is it that torture has not so far been used on the prisoner?"

Brother Athangild answered: "Your Reverence is forgetting, in your praiseworthy zeal, that we have only just reached the stage of individual cross-examination, and that this meeting was convened precisely in order to discuss that point."

Brother Bernard intervened and asked that his words should appear in the records *ipsis verbis*. And he turned significantly to the scribe sitting at a desk at the back of the room:

"We cannot, reverend brothers, prejudge any evidence. We are not here to discuss whether or not torture should already have been used or to deliberate upon whether it *should* be used. Our humble duty is merely the rigorous application of the Regulations, which operate independently of us, setting out, determining and classifying the successive stages of a trial. I repeat: I wish to make it clear that it is not up to us to decide on the matter of torture, the prisoner makes that decision by his show of obstinacy."

Brother Demetrios asked permission to speak:

"Brothers, if you will allow me, the question we must ask ourselves is this: is the prisoner persisting in his negative obstinacy or not, and if he is, is he thus standing in the way of the trial reaching a conclusion?"

"Exactly, that is the only question," said Brother Anthony in a tiny voice that seemed to emerge from beneath the vast table. "I will put it to the vote. Anyone who agrees, stay as you are. Anyone who disagrees, raise your right hand."

"I protest, Your Reverence," cried Brother Bernard. "A point of order. A point of order. Your Reverence cannot put to the vote a proposal that has not been clearly formulated!"

"I am the only one who has the right to protest," exclaimed Brother Demetrios angrily, "because I was the person who formulated the proposal. And it was, I understand, so clearly formulated that our Reverend Brother Anthony immediately accepted it."

"*Distinguo*," said Brother Athangild. "And I remind your Reverences, venerable brothers, that neither of those protests is valid, nor is any other proposal or vote. Because we need to know one thing which we do not know: how is it that a man endowed by the Devil with such immense powers, a man who," and here he made the sign of the cross, "enjoys the Devil's society and protection, how is it that he cannot set himself free, indeed, the swine has not even tried to do so? What evil can the Prince of Darkness be plotting by abandoning him for all these years?"

Brother Bermudo let out a guffaw and said:

"Your Reverence's question shows that your knowledge of heretical matters blinds you to the unfathomable ways in which heinous sins are satisfied." And he added smugly: "The Devil may be enjoying the prisoner's sufferings, and the prisoner himself may be enjoying his sufferings and the pleasure the Devil is taking in them. Does our Reverend Brother Anthony agree that such a thing is indeed possible for the infernal powers."

Brother Anthony merely nodded, solemnly and discreetly.

Brother Bernard then said: "I have a suggestion to put to the tribunal. If the physical torture of the prisoner could contribute to increasing his obstinacy, and making the Devil, witnessing this, only laugh at us all the more, I propose... Your Reverences know that the torments of human love are great, especially if the flesh is contaminated with vice. If the Devil is particularly enamoured of the prisoner, he will doubtless suffer to see that the prisoner still loves the woman with whom he most sinned. The sins of both of them are doubtless pleasing to him, and he himself instigated them. However, the torments of human love and those of divine love are not pleasing to him, and I can quote chapter and verse on that. Let the prisoner remain where he is, and let the tribunal observe his behaviour when we transfer Dona Urraca to his cell."

A murmur of scandalised disapproval ran round the table. And Brother Athangild spoke for all the others when he said: "Am I, are we all, hearing correctly? Is my Reverend Brother actually proposing to allow the two lead prisoners to sin again within these pure and hallowed walls?"

But Brother Bermudo intervened: "Is Your Reverence forgetting the efficacy of the chastity belt, the male version, that this tribunal so prudently fitted to the prisoner? I agree with the proposal, as long as Dona Urraca wears a similar belt, because, after all, one never knows…"

The tiny voice of Brother Anthony interrupted him:

"She already has one. It's in the Regulations."

… …

When the door swung open, he, as usual, did not move. And only when the door closed again without anyone having spoken, did he raise his head. After his years in prison, his eyes could clearly see the light coming in through the bars, but he could also see huge shadows, those of the monks, which he knew all too well. He lowered his head again, and did not even move when the mouse touched his foot. The mouse climbed up his foot and felt his ankle. It wasn't a mouse, it was a hand. He looked up then and saw before him a crouching shadow with long, dishevelled hair, both of whose hands were feeling their way up his legs as far as his knees. He reached out his arms to her and, with a great clanking of chains, he lay down. She lay down next to him, and there they stayed, utterly still and locked in an embrace. The members of the tribunal observed this absolute immobility. Suddenly, a shudder ran through the two prisoners and a hoarse cry echoed round the cell. And such was the tribunal's confidence in the official and infallible chastity belts that it did not even occur to them that the couple had possessed each other. Silence and immobility were soon restored. And as if nothing had happened, the door was opened and the monks came back in. The two shapes on the floor were a tangle of chains and remained where they were, still locked in an embrace and utterly still. Two guards bent down to separate them. It was easy enough to remove the one who wasn't chained: a limp body that they dragged out into the corridor followed by a troop of monks. It wasn't just a limp body, it was a corpse. But it wasn't Dona Urraca. Or it was. But the long hair was fair and the dead features were his.

The monks fell to their knees, making the sign of the cross, trembling and uttering conjurations, while all one heard of the guards was the sound of fleeing feet.

VIII

The tribunal then began torturing him. They began by shaving his head and then shaving off the long beard that had grown during his incarceration. They submitted him to the rack and the wheel, then tried strappado, red-hot pincers and a metal-tipped flail. His thin body full of sores, its limbs all dislocated, was a ruin that crawled at the feet of the judges, unable to speak, uttering only grunts. All his youth and beauty had vanished. It was in this state that he was brought before the other accused, male and female, one by one, but even they did not recognise him. Even the three principal maidens, their hair now turned a grubby white, showed no sign of recognising that torn rag of a man, who had to be held upright. It was in this state that the chaplain and the physicians were brought before him; seated on a litter, naked from the waist down and shrivelled and burned like torches, these were the men who had been the first to accuse him and, some time later, to provide the first proof. The torturers experimented with various ways of putting the prisoner's hat on his head, but not once did he become invisible. An interesting detail, though, every time they put the hat on his head, he defecated, and the excrement ran down his legs. Just to make sure, the monks repeated the experiment in the most diverse situations, with Brother Anthony and Brother Demetrios feverishly taking notes.

On the last occasion, the experiments went on until late in the night, and the two monks, having dispensed with the prisoner, were still busily comparing notes, when, suddenly, Brother Anthony shot a terrified, incredulous glance at Brother Demetrios, unable to believe what he was seeing.

They started suspiciously back from each other, frozen in fear. Each one took up a candle and studied the other's face. Even beneath their hoods, they could see that they both now bore the fair, youthful, resplendent face they had destroyed.

They fled to their respective cells in terror. And the following day, they did not attend the tribunal meeting.

As the oldest of the monks, Brother Bermudo took Brother Anthony's place, having been told that both Brother Anthony and the "enemy of alchemy" had been taken ill. However, when they were about to begin discussing the order of the day, he saw a look of horror on the faces of Brother Athangild and Brother Bernard. Even the scribe at the back of the room was craning his neck to get a better view.

Brother Bernard leapt to his feet, ran to the end of the table, crying: "Holy Virgin have mercy on us!" and hurriedly pulled Brother Bermudo's hood over his head. Brother Bermudo protested and struggled. And Brother Athangild howled out an order for the scribe to leave the room. Then he ran over to Brother Bernard and, stammering, tried to get him to cover his head too. But Brother Bernard, releasing Brother Bermudo, who was staring at him in bewilderment, then did the same with Brother Athangild's hood. The three of them stood facing each other, all with their hoods on. And Brother Athangild said:

"This is what must have happened to the others, and that's why they didn't come to the meeting."

Making sure the door was firmly closed and bolted from the inside, Brother Bernard said:

"We must finish this trial as quickly as possible. If not, that face will appear on the face of anyone who ever saw it, and there's hardly anyone who hasn't."

Brother Bernard exclaimed: "But what about the Regulations?"

And Brother Athangild said: "Forget the Regulations. This is a public emergency. It's like the plague. Hang and burn that man today. And let everyone else shut themselves up in the leper's hospital."

Pulling their hoods down over their eyes, they went in search of the other two monks. Together they decided that the gallows and the pyre should be set up in the courtyard of the palace itself, for which they would only need to ask permission from the archbishop. The latter received them with his hood pulled well down over his eyes and immediately gave his permission.

The prisoner would be hanged first, then disembowelled, and his body immediately burned on the pyre that would have been lit meanwhile. Disembowelment was essential to ensure that there would be no possibility of any demoniacal resurrection before the wretched body was burned. He would be hanged as he was, in his chains, just in case he should suddenly become invisible again and because the chains would add weight, thus avoiding the need for the hangman to go too close to him before he was dead. Everyone except the prisoner would wear a hood.

They had to carry him on a stretcher into the courtyard, but, by then, night had already fallen, because the erection of the gallows and the preparation of the pyre had taken far longer than expected. During that time, the five monks had been frenetically engaged in removing the other prisoners from the palace. By torchlight, they dragged the body over to the gallows. Since the prisoner could not stand, the hangman fastened a noose around his chest and under his armpits, and his assistant pulled hard until the body was hanging in the air, the long chains dangling. Then, straddling the crossbeam, the executioner slipped the noose proper over the prisoner's head and let out a cry.

The small group of hooded figures looked up anxiously. What could be the problem? The executioner, also hooded, climbed down to explain. He could not possibly hang the prisoner while the latter still had the iron collar around his neck. They would have to take it off first.

This caused great anxiety and perplexity. They set off into town in search of the duty blacksmith, but he was nowhere to be found. Meanwhile, the assistant was still holding on to the other rope and asked if he was going to have to continue waiting there, because although the body itself weighed almost nothing, the chains were very heavy. They told him he could let go, which he immediately did, and with a clang and clatter of chains, the body collapsed onto the platform in a heap of flesh and iron. Finally, the blacksmith arrived, and, in the silence, all you could hear was him hammering away, until the collar finally fell off.

The body was hauled up again, the chains still dangling loose, and the executioner slipped the noose around the prisoner's neck. The local catchpole then clapped his hands, the assistant released the body, and the executioner jumped onto the hanged man's shoulders. The body spun round, setting the chains swaying, and then continued to hang there, turning slowly. From beneath the assembled hoods came a sigh of relief.

However, the executioner, clinging to the rope, leaned forward to look at the head between his knees. Then, several times, he hoisted himself up and slammed back down again onto the prisoner's shoulders. At last, clambering off the gallows, his bare torso running with sweat, he sat despairingly on the edge of the platform.

The hooded ones came running over to him.

"He's not dead. He won't die. Every time I bear down on him," and here he made the sign of the cross, "someone raises him up."

They did not even have to exchange a glance to understand what was going on. And Brother Anthony then made an important decision.

IX

Brother Anthony of Salzburg shut himself up in the room he had occupied since being appointed by Rome to come to Cologne and lead the tribunal. It was a large room, far larger than suited the ascetic tastes of its occupant, who could, however, console himself with the cold draughts coming in through the gaps round the window and door and the wind whipping down the chimney, for he never ordered the fire to be lit. However, just then, the size of the room suited him, because he needed space for what he was about to attempt.

Kneeling at the prayer desk, he prepared himself by praying with his eyes fixed on the crucifix. Then he got up, made the sign of the cross, took the crucifix off the wall and placed it in a corner upside down and with the image turned to face the whitewashed wall. He saw that the shadow cast by the crucifix, however distorted, was still that of a cross. And so he picked up the crucifix again and placed it in the same position at the back of the empty fireplace. He then removed his own episcopal cross, which he placed on the table, face down. When he took off his hood and his habit, he looked even more diminutive in his baggy hemp shirt. Crouching by his bed, he pulled out from under it a bundle of books. He took one, opened it and placed it on the table so that the bound spine lay on his episcopal cross. Then he leafed slowly through the book, squinting slightly so as to make out the red letters on the yellowing parchment. He took a candle and placed that on top of the book. He then rolled his shirt up to his waist and tied a knot in it so that it would not slip down and, reading quietly from the book, he spat onto the four corners of the table before wetting his fingers with saliva and anointing himself on those parts that the Devil most tempts and that most tempt the Devil. Every time he bent down, he had to push back his long, fair hair, which felt very strange to him after his many tonsured years. The same thing happened when he crawled around the table, tracing a circle in spit. Then he began to read out the invocations in a loud voice. The louder he spoke, the more his voice quavered and cracked, but the invocations themselves rang out loud and clear.

He repeated them three times. Nothing happened. He repeated them again. Nothing. Then wiggling his bottom, he danced around the table and repeated the invocations. Nothing.

"*Veni, veni, veni, imundo spirto, veni, veni, veni, spirto imundo, veni, veni, veni, creator, imperator, absileus, pontifex, sanctus et sutcnas, sanctus et sutcnas, sanctus et sutcnas.*"

Nothing.

He clapped the book shut.

"In the name of the Father, the Son and the Holy Ghost, O Unholy Spirit, O Prince of Darkness, Lord of Evil, Dispenser of Glory, Guardian of Souls, I summon you.

"What do you want?" said a voice almost in his ear. And he felt a body brush against his.

Brother Anthony drew back and, turning to where the voice

had come from, said:

"First, I want you to show yourself so that we can talk."

"You need to see me in order to talk to me?"

Brother Anthony did not respond, he merely waited.

A shadow began to thicken beside him and to take on human form, but went no further than that.

"Is that enough?" asked the voice.

"No."

"So you think I gave you my face, do you, and want to see it for yourself?" And the voice tittered.

"I know you have no face and that you put on whichever face suits you, but I summoned you and you will appear."

The shadow grew lighter and became a transparent patch of light.

"How's this?"

"Come, Satan, show yourself as you are!"

The light suddenly vanished, and before Brother Anthony stood a monk just like him, with his body and with the face that had been his before the change.

"Is this all right?"

"Fine."

"So what do you want from me?"

"I want you to tell me, for the love of Christ, why the evil man whom we condemned to death cannot die."

"Will you accept my answer?"

"Yes."

"Because I am madly in love with him and have been ever since I first laid eyes on him. And I will not allow him to be destroyed. During all these years, I have tried in vain to show you that I would not allow it. And when you tried to tempt him with temptation itself, when his image was about to be lost because the woman would certainly not resist his embrace, I punished you."

"But who are you to punish the punishers?"

"As you yourself said: I am Prince of the Darkness that is my domain, Lord of the Evil I rule over, Dispenser of the Glory I administer, Guardian of the Souls I conquer."

"You mean that we cannot kill him, and that he is immortal because you desire him?"

"No, he is immortal because that is what *you* desire. Don't you understand, I could have his soul instantly, if it was his soul I wanted. But I don't want his soul. And do you know why? *Because he has no soul.* How can I want something that does not exist? I only want *things* or what can become a thing. Anything that does not exist is not my business. And he, he is indestructible beauty, indestructible youth, the indestructible power of love. Why do you think you were able to capture him? It was because, for a moment, he grew weary and began to acquire a soul or what you call a soul and which I amuse myself devouring. But you have no idea how adorable he is, how innocent, how far he is from your grasp or mine. I know your frailties and the temptations to which you have succumbed, yes, I know that, and you know that I know, but you will never understand how I have loved him and how I have suffered for him. But he never ever returned my love."

"You're lying."

"I am, but only out of a kind of modesty. It's not what you think, though. He only gave himself to me twice, once when he thought I was the love he did not know and once, and this was really the only time, because he wanted to rid himself of the anxiety provoked by the soul growing inside him."

"What do you want from him, then?"

"Nothing. Strange though it may seem, nothing. I want him to live, I want him to go out and about in the world using his powers and for me to be a witness to his eternal life."

"And if we grant him his freedom, if we let him go, do you promise that everything will go back to how it was before?"

"That depends."

"Depends on what?"

"Exactly, it depends. If you set him free and shelve the whole trial, which is easy enough, because it's been going on for so many years now that you yourself were not among the first to judge him, I will restore to you your ugly, would-be virtuous faces and look forward to seeing you in Hell. That is all I can promise."

"And what about punishing evil, punishing sins?"

"My child," and he placed on the monk's shoulder a hand of fire that singed his hemp shirt, "how ignorant you are. I am the one who punishes evil."

Brother Anthony could not help but smile.

"Yes, me. Who else do you think is in your body and in your mind when you deal out justice, however just? Me, of course. Which is why I am quite right to call you 'my son'."

"So what shall we agree?"

"Good, now you are being reasonable – and intelligent too. Even my power has its limits. Oh, not the limits you imagine and preach about, but other far more complicated ones that you could never even fathom. And to tell the truth, neither can I. I have told you what I can promise."

"So be it." And Brother Anthony held out his hand to himself.

The other him shook his hand (a hand even colder than his own) and said: "It's a deal." And Satan was already beginning to change back into a transparent mist, when he returned briefly to his former shape and added: "As for rolling up your shirt, my son, you have obviously never looked at yourself in the mirror. It really wasn't worth the bother." And with a snigger he was gone.

Brother Anthony glanced down at himself, quickly adjusted his shirt and donned his habit again. He hid the book under the bed, along with the others. He put on his episcopal cross, hung the crucifix back in its place and knelt before it to say a brief prayer. Then, pulling on his hood, he went downstairs into the courtyard.

Everything was as he had left it in the torchlight. The body and the chains lying in a heap on the platform. The executioner sitting on the edge of the platform. The assistant standing nearby. His hooded brothers waiting between the gallows and the pyre.

Brother Anthony went over to them. They knelt down, and he said:

"Unchain that man. Give him some clothes to wear. Put him on a horse and lead him out of town."

The other monks hesitated. Brother Anthony declared:

"If we do that, God will grant us a miracle. I know this for a fact."

The blacksmith cut through the shackles around the prisoner's wrists and ankles and waist (and the tinkling noise he made seemed never-ending). Then he removed the chastity belt. The body lying at the feet of the five monks was like one large wound, a vast stinking pustule.

Brother Anthony ordered them to pick him up and apply some ointment to his wounds.

They did so.

Brother Anthony turned then and said in his shrill, strident voice:

"In God's name, I declare that anyone, cleric or not, who speaks of what he saw here tonight will be condemned by this tribunal to having his eyes gouged out, his tongue cut out and his hands lopped off. We hanged this man, we disembowelled him, we burned him. You are all witnesses to this. Clothe him and put him on a horse."

Over his shaven head they slipped a sack with holes in it, the sort they give to lepers, and tried in vain to make him stay in the saddle on the horse they had brought for him. He kept slipping off and falling to the ground.

Brother Anthony changed his mind.

"Leave him there. Let's go." And when, followed by the others, he was about to walk through the great arch leading to the stairs, he turned and said: "Leave the doors open."

In the dark, deserted courtyard, the body lay stretched out on the ground, at the foot of the gallows.

X

When the five monks were gathered together in the council room and the doors firmly shut, Brother Anthony adamantly refused to explain to the others what had happened during his secret interview. No amount of dogged questioning, no insinuations could wring from him anything other than a declaration that it had been the only way of restoring order, because, while he was at prayer, he had received a visitation, and from his conversation with that visitor, he had concluded that the Enemy, filthy swine, refused to receive that awkward creature in his domain.

Brother Demetrios thought this impossible, not to mention a sin against the Holy Spirit, to declare, a priori, that any soul, even one guilty of the most heinous of sins, was irredeemable. How, then, could one allow that such a soul was inevitably condemned to Hell?

Brother Anthony, who had cringed at the word "soul", made no attempt to conceal his furious impatience. "Enough of your scholastic nitpicking. How could such a soul be condemned to Hell if the Devil himself did not want him?"

Brushing aside his colleague's impatience with a superior smile, Brother Demetrios went on: "If the Devil doesn't want him, ergo that same Devil must know that, once the creature in question is dead, he will have to receive his soul. Now, given that the infernal powers are, by nature, contradictory, ergo…"

"Damn your ergos!" Brother Anthony cried, and his voice hissed with fury: "Your Reverence may know all about heretics, but as for those infernal powers…" and here he made the sign of the cross… "I know all about them. If Your Reverence is inclined to dispute that view, then…" And his eyes flashed so fiercely that he needed no words to complete his threat.

For some moments, Brother Demetrios remained frozen and silent, then he muttered: "It would seem that not only does Your Reverence understand them, you would also appear to have reached an understanding with them."

A shudder ran through everyone present, and even Brother Demetrios trembled at what he had said.

However, Brother Anthony closed his eyes, provisionally dedicated his colleague's future humiliation to God, and concluded the discussion by saying with a sour smile:

"Do Your Reverences wish to keep the faces that the Devil gave you or regain those given to you by Our Lord God?"

Brother Bernard found the courage to make a joke:

"May God forgive me, but our new faces would certainly serve us better."

The other hooded monks were filled with indignation, and Brother Demetrios even exchanged a knowing look of condemnation with Brother Anthony.

Brother Bernard went on in a rather different tone:

"At least when Our Lady is gracious enough to visit me, what with her being so beautiful, at least I would have a face worthier of…"

"Heavens!" exclaimed the others. And Brother Athangild cried:

"Do you realise what you are saying? That a devil's face would be worthier of the Virgin?"

"I didn't say that. All I meant was that a beautiful face, illuminated by Grace, would be a face in which Grace shone still more brightly…"

"Anathema! Anathema! Brother Anthony! Brother Bernard has fallen into a grave error. And this tribunal should judge him. How can a man who has been present at the lofty decisions made by this holy tribunal be allowed to get away with such a grave heresy? I denounce him as a heretic."

Aflame with indignation, Brother Athangild pointed the finger at Brother Bernard, who shrank back, and as he did so, his hood slipped off to reveal his beautiful fair hair and fine face.

He immediately covered his head, and the others remained stiff and safely hooded. Brother Anthony rang the bell.

The door opened and in came two guards.

Brother Anthony pointed at Brother Bernard and said:

"Take that man away and keep him incommunicado. Let no one speak to him!"

When the door closed, Brother Athangild sat down glumly, his head in his hands, and said:

"Who would have thought that a man held to be a saint should now be condemned irremissably to go to Hell." And he sighed.

The other three hooded monks trembled. Brother Demetrios again shot a sideways glance at Brother Anthony and murmured:

"I draw the tribunal's attention to the words just spoken by Brother Athangild and which throw considerable doubt on the

Christian charity of a man known as the 'hammer of heretics'. He has prejudged the salvation or perdition of a soul without taking into account divine Grace."

Brother Anthony rang the bell. And two hooded guards came in. Brother Anthony indicated Brother Athangild, and the guards led him away.

The three remaining monks sat silent and unmoving.

Then Brother Bermudo said: "It's madness what we're doing, utter madness."

Brother Anthony asked: "What are you calling 'madness'? The solution to this affair? The inquiry that became necessary in order to root out evil ideas from the minds of our reverend brothers? The trial? Respect for the Regulations that have always guided us? Perhaps Your Reverence could tell me..." and his hand hovered over the bell.

Brother Bermudo did not reply. And Brother Demetrios asked:

"Do you think he's still there?"

The other two hooded figures turned to him. And Brother Anthony got up and ran to the window that gave onto the courtyard. Their view was blocked, however, by the pyre, with its pile of firewood and the broom scattered all around. Followed by the other two monks, Brother Anthony ran into the next room. They could not see from there either. In the moonlight, the dark shadow of the gallows fell on the very spot where he would be lying. All three of them forced open the door to the room beyond and rushed to the window. They now had a clear view of the place where they had left him. He was not there.

They turned back and ran, panting, lifting up their habits so that they could run faster. They hurtled down the main staircase, but at the archway to the courtyard, they stopped. He was near the tunnel that led out into the square and was slowly, painfully dragging himself along like someone climbing a very steep slope.

They ran a few steps, then stopped short, aware of the clatter of their sandals on the paving stones. Still holding up their habits, they tiptoed forward until they reached the end of the tunnel, where they stood watching.

But he stopped too. And there they all stayed: he like a corpse lying face down as if caught in the act of escaping, and the three monks hunched in the archway, holding their breath.

The sky was beginning to get light, and the courtyard walls were gradually growing paler, while the windows of corridors and rooms grew blacker. The paving stones looked as if they were covered by a milky white dampness.

Brother Demetrios murmured: "What shall we do? Leave him there until it's daylight and people in the palace start moving around?"

Brother Anthony straightened up and thought. Then he said:

"Reverend brothers, you are going to help him up so that he can walk, however feebly, and take him wherever he wishes to go."

From beneath their hoods, the others stared at him in horror, or so Brother Anthony thought.

Brother Anthony added: "I will follow you with my crucifix in my hand."

The others hesitated, but Brother Anthony gave them an imperious shove. They went over to the body and managed to get him to his feet very easily, because he was much lighter than they had imagined. They advanced along the tunnel to the palace gate. The guards, half-asleep, were startled at the sight. However, they immediately recognised the diminutive figure of Brother Anthony, who, holding up his crucifix, waved them away.

The group stopped in the large square outside, because the men supporting him had no sense of where the battered body, its feet dragging along the ground, wanted to go.

They consulted each other on what to do next, and decided to try different directions and see how he reacted. They advanced in zigzag fashion, each time facing one of the four ways out of the square. Still he did not react. They stopped.

Brother Anthony ordered them to lay him down on the ground. And they stood behind him, waiting for him to move. In the morning light - a very pink and white light that cast a glittering golden dust over the tall dark buildings in the square and sent a low breeze gusting over the ground – the body, even though it was face down, was a truly horrible sight. Its shaven head was covered in dark bruises and pustules, and the wound on the throat was like a bungled decapitation that had left the head only barely connected to the body. Indeed, you could not really see the body, covered as it was in sacking, but you could get a sense of it from the arms and legs in which the bones were visible beneath a tight skin full of purulent lacerations. The hands, all tendons and protuberant bones, were particularly horrible, the fingers made to look exaggeratedly long by the twisted, broken, overgrown nails. And as if separated from the arms and legs by the ulcerated circle left by the iron fetters, both hands and feet looked as if they had been half-severed too.

XI

The sun began to flood into the square through the streets on the eastern side and, suddenly, it struck the buildings full on and lit up the entire square with a silvery orange light. The very long shadows cast by the three monks fell across the body. Brother Anthony turned away, and the others did the same. And they continued to wait. The body, on which the sun was now beating down, remained motionless. At one point, it seemed to the monks that it moaned. And they listened still more carefully. It must have been an illusion. Then it seemed to them that the body moved very slightly, that a tremor ran through it, the way the skin of horses quivers when bitten by flies. However, the body was so still that any such tremor was out of the question. Even the breathing was imperceptible. Had the man died?

It was then that the hands moved. The fingers clenched and unclenched, clenched and unclenched, then stopped. Then, with a superhuman effort, one of the knees bent and the body rolled over slightly, so that it was half lying on its side. The monks, in unison, uttered a muffled cry that echoed round the square like a breaking wave. Startled, they turned to look behind them. The square was full of people, forming a dense, silent, unmoving mass. Brother Anthony held up his crucifix and cried:

"He has the plague, run!"

Then he made the sign of the cross. ·

The crowd did not move.

"Didn't you hear me? The man has the plague. Run. Get out of here. Go back to your houses. That is an order. In the name of the Holy Father, as God's representative, I order you: go back to your houses on pain of excommunication!"

The crowd maintained its silence, then, as one, took a step forward, forcing Brother Anthony to retreat, shouting: "The man has the plague. Run!"

Instead, the crowd, whose breathing sounded now like a rushing river, took another step, and Brother Anthony again retreated, saying in a faint, tremulous voice: "You are all excommunicated forthwith. May God's curse fall on you and on your children!"

The crowd took yet another step and, very slowly, began to walk. When Brother Anthony turned, afraid he might stumble, he saw that the body, its drooping head invisible between its shoulders, was gradually, on all fours, heading for one of the streets leading out of the square, with, behind him, the other two monks.

Thus they left the square and entered a street leading downhill, the body creeping painfully forward and leaving a trail of blood, followed by the two monks and then Brother Anthony, who alternated between trying to keep pace with them and turning to look back at the crowd, which was now like a sea of slow, thick lava flowing between the walls of the street. More people kept emerging from the houses along the way, and the cortège continued on, flanked by still more people, who were all gradually absorbed into the sea of lava. Apart from the sound of breathing and shuffling feet, the slow, dense wave was utterly silent. The only voice to be heard was that of Brother Anthony, who, in hoarse, strident tones, would occasionally, mechanically shout: "The man has the plague, you hear, the plague! Run!"

Where the streets crossed other streets, fresh crowds were waiting in silence to join the cortège, but it was no longer just one mass moving down that one street. At each crossing, it was clear that down the other streets running more or less parallel similar rivers were flowing, equally slow and silent, their gentle rumble hovering above the crowd and above the town. Ahead, though, there was no one. And the body continued crawling slowly along, first a hand, then a knee.

Now and then, a woman would rush out from a doorway or from the crowd, crouch down between the body and the two monks following immediately behind and would mop up with a rag any drops of blood on the paving stones.

Whenever the body stopped, the procession would stop too. And during one of those pauses, Brother Bermudo stumbled and fell. The body, however, continued on its way. Brother Demetrios followed behind. And whenever Brother Anthony turned round, he could see Brother Bermudo's fallen form disappearing beneath the feet of the crowd.

The cortège was still moving and had now reached the gates of the city, through which the body crawled, still on all fours. Beyond the walls, while the body continued on down, the crowd spread out like dammed-up water allowed to flow freely again. Not entirely freely though because the sides of the road were now seething with people who had doubtless come from the outskirts of the city and the nearest villages, and all flowed seamlessly into the sea emerging from the city gates.

The body continued to advance, having turned off along a narrow path. Then – and at this, a murmur rippled across the fields black with people – the body raised itself up into a kneeling position. Then it placed one hand on the ground, brought the opposite leg forwards, planted one foot on the ground and stood up. It swayed slowly and seemed about to fall. But no. Dragging its feet and, as though being in permanent danger of falling forward actually helped, it took several steps before falling face first next to a large ditch.

Then, as the body again began dragging itself along, it toppled over and rolled into the ditch where it lay helpless on its back, revealing the sores left by the chains around the waist and by the chastity belt. And lit by the noonday sun, the face was horrible to see, possibly even more so than the rest of the body: the wide, hollow eyes, the broken nose, the mouth gaping open to show a swollen tongue and toothless gums, and the whole head, like the face itself, a mass of bruises, purple and black.

The body stayed there for a long time, with the crowd pressed together along the length of the ditch, with which all were familiar. Standing on the edge of the ditch, Brother Anthony and Brother Demetrios could feel the crowd pressing from behind, while on the other side waited another sea of people.

Then moans and sobs began to emerge from the supine, splayed body. Brother Anthony held his crucifix higher above the ditch only to have it snatched so violently from his hands that its gold chain broke. The crying grew louder, a wordless lament, a loud litany that spread to the vast throng.

First, two men, then others, leapt into the ditch and began

scrabbling with their hands. It was as if they were being guided by the ever more piercing cries. Then, suddenly, a great silence fell. A lock of blonde hair emerged from beneath the earth, then a putrefying head, which, in the men's eagerness to disinter it, almost became detached from the body that then began to appear as well.

The men drew back. And the body rolled over again and dragged itself towards the exposed corpse, which must once have been a woman's. When the body touched the corpse with one of its long, long hands, they all saw how the hair on the skull became black and the corpse itself became an astonishingly beautiful woman.

The body fell back beside her and, gradually, as its breathing became louder and more stertorous, its wounds began to vanish, its hair grew fair again, its features regained their vanished beauty. And at the very moment when everyone present saw that he had died, he resembled a god.

For a long time, they all stood utterly still. Then the men bent down and tried to pick up the two bodies in order to carry them elsewhere. Impossible. They sweated and heaved, but it was impossible. Then, by using their shirts as a kind of sling, they tried to lift both together. This proved equally impossible.

From the other side of the ditch, a woman threw in a handful of earth. The men jumped out. It did not take long for the ditch to be filled and for the banks on either side to be gone.

It was all over, thought Brother Anthony, but still the crowd did not move, waiting for something.

And from the place where the pair were lying a tiny plant began to sprout, growing larger as they watched. It was already about three feet high when the buds opened, greeted by a great clamour from the crowd. The buds became huge, round red roses that gave off an intoxicating perfume. It was a strange perfume, not like the scent of a rose, no, it was the perfume of... Brother Anthony grabbed the plant and tried to uproot it. He managed to break off just one stem, and out of the wound ran two threads of liquid. One was a whitish resin, the other a red sap. Brother Anthony stood, eyes and mouth agape, not even noticing that his still extended hand was becoming black and shrivelled.

And the reason he had no time to notice this was because his skull had been bashed in, and the crowd were dragging him and Brother Demetrios, by the feet, back to the city.

XII

For days and days, the city divided into groups, there were more disturbances, more assaults, more fires, and long processions filed in pilgrimage down to the miraculous rose bush. The streets were full of debris and unburied bodies. In the main square, the fire in the archbishop's palace had spread to other buildings. The same had happened in other areas, and the city looked as if it had been the victim of a great military raid. In the midst of all this, though, the population behaved as if life were a wild feast of pleasures, and the various groups that formed the processions heading off to visit the rosebush came directly from those many banquets and orgies.

One day, on leaving a banquet, a man, who happened to be one of those who had tried to carry the two prodigious corpses back to the city, stumbled and fell in the street. People thought he was drunk, but no, he had the plague. His body was soon covered with buboes and he died within a matter of hours. Cases of plague proliferated with giddying speed. People collapsed and were left unburied. Processions were made to the rosebush, with everyone carrying lilies, singing and praying.

However, the victims of plague dropped to the ground right next to the rosebush and the processions dispersed in panic.

In carts, on horseback, or escaping as best they could, the survivors abandoned the city, which was gradually overrun by crows, wolves and wild cats. Weeds sprang up among the ruins, while the wind and the dust took turns to sweep away the ashes and the bones and to cover everything.

Alone, at the bottom of the hill, the great rosebush, untouched by either the winds or the winter rains, continued to flourish and flower, almost like a small, perfumed tree.

… …

Anyone walking the city's deserted streets, would have little idea of what had happened there if he or she had no personal experience of such devastation. For the rebellion and the plague born there had travelled all round the world and unleashed destruction on a scale never seen before. No castle or palace could be said to have escaped, however far they were from any roads. Not even a certain small, white castle near the banks of a river, once occupied by the soldiers of the Holy Office. Singing the romance-cum-ballad about roses of blood and milk, which had become a kind of anthem of rebellion among the people, the rebels had made a huge bonfire, hurling everything out into the courtyard, including a vast bed that had been flung from a window.

Dancing in a circle around the fire, carrying soldiers' heads impaled on spears, they were all chanting:

> *Death to the bishop and death to the pope,*
> *Death to all the clergy.*

Ah, roses made of milk and blood
That only the earth would drink!
Death to the monks and death to the nuns,
Death to all their papishness.
Ah, roses made of blood and milk
That only the earth would drink!
Death to the king and death to the count,
Death to all the nobility.
Ah, roses made of milk and blood
That only the earth would drink!
Death to the judges and the hangman too,
Death to all the judiciary.
Ah, roses made of blood and milk
That only the earth would drink!
Death to all buyers and all sellers too,
Death to all of usury.
Ah, roses made of milk and blood
That only the earth would drink!
Death to fathers and death to sons,
Death to all domesticity.
Ah, roses made of blood and milk
That only the earth would drink!
Death to husbands and death to wives,
Death to conjugality.
Ah, roses made of milk and blood
That only the earth would drink!
Death to friends and death to lovers,
Death to all such squandered love.
Ah, roses made of blood and milk,
That only the earth would drink!
Death to everything, death to all,
But life, long life to the people's revolution.

Jorge de Sena

Ah, roses made of milk and blood
That only the earth would drink!

… … … … … … … … … … … … … … … … … … … …

Bands of runaway children and youths, abandoned and starving, wandered the fields and the roads, killing and stealing and dropping dead from cold and hunger. Others from the ruined cities and towns immediately replaced them, swelling those scattered hordes that aimlessly traversed vast distances. In the deserted farms, they slept huddled up together to keep warm; and, sometimes, if night surprised them while they were still on the road, they would sleep out in the open. At daybreak, leaving behind those who had died and who had even served as blankets to the living, they would resume their march.

And thus it was that two of those bands arrived simultaneously at the ruins of a town and at those of a castle.

The band that reached the castle crossed the rotting drawbridge and went into the courtyard. There, some investigated the empty stables, while others went up the steps and found themselves in an enormous room, at the far end of which was a door or, rather, the burned remains of its frame. The next room was a heap of rubble fallen from the upper floors of the tower in which it stood. Jumping over the scorched beams and stones, they ran into the other rooms. And in the middle of one of these, where the roof had not

The ones who came upon the town explored all the abandoned houses until they reached the main square. There, some went off exploring the surrounding buildings, while others went down a tunnel that led into the palace. In the vast courtyard stood a gallows from which a small, shrivelled corpse with a shattered skull hung suspended on a chain. They amused themselves throwing stones at the corpse, and when one foot came loose and fell off, they played with it, tossing it from one to the other. However, they entirely fallen in, they came upon the remains of a large dismantled bathtub, in which they each took turns pretending to bathe. Then they came running back to the room that was filled with rubble. And then, where the wall was paler despite the scorch marks, as if a bed had once stood there, they rolled around on the floor, screaming wildly, feeling their bodies burning. They rushed out then and, leaving the castle, raced through the devastated forest to the river. And tearing off their clothes in the first clearing they came to, they jumped into the water.

quickly grew bored and ran over to the great arch leading into the palace, where they went up the stairs and walked through room after room, jumping over the rubble fallen from the upper storeys. In one room they found what was left of a long table, half destroyed by fire, and on the floor, in one corner, an iron chest lay open on its side. When they moved it, two huge black spiders emerged, lifting their arched legs, and the children promptly trod on them. Some crouched down to get a better look, and one, braver than the others, put his hand inside the chest and brought out a grubby, faded piece of cloth that must once have been a hat. They fought furiously over the hat, until one of them got hold of it and, as a sign that it was his, put it on his head and vanished like smoke.

After bathing in the river, they lay down in the shade. When the other boy had disappeared, they had all felt too terrified to move. However, the burning sensation did not stop. Then they felt someone slapping them, tugging at their hair, tearing off their clothes. Lying in the shade, they began to fight each other, simply out of an urge to do something. When the first one summoned up the courage to flee, the others followed in hot pursuit. When they heard a noise coming from the forest, it had already become clear that the urge was not just to fight. They raced down the steps, while beside them, stones from up above rolled down of their own accord. Panting hard, they could make out among the trees a small cart being drawn along by an old man and a young woman. They ran across the courtyard, their footsteps clattering down the tunnel, where they were pursued by loud guffaws. In their naked state, they approached the old man and the young woman, who stopped, astonished. The boys continued out into the square and disappeared down the road, while the other boy, who had reappeared now, smiling broadly, waved to them with his hat. They surrounded the cart and the small group composed of the old man and the young woman. As if he were dancing, he zigzagged down the path. And while some overturned the cart, kicking away the few possessions it contained, others were beating the old man, while others were dragging the young woman away and tearing off her clothes. He reached the city gate and when he couldn't see the others, he felt alone and anxious. One after the other, they raped her. Looking around to see if he could see them, he continued down the hill. They left her unconscious on the ground and went back to where they had left the tattered clothes they had been wearing. Either he was alone, or the others were hiding somewhere: but no one would catch him unawares again, he would be sure to see them first: he again put on the hat. Silently, without looking at each other, they pulled on their clothes and went on their way. He was invisible when he came upon a huge rose bush with huge roses that gave off a strong scent, and there he stayed. The whole mob was walking along, side by side, in silence, until one of them stopped, grabbed another boy by the arm and nodded and winked at him: the other boy burst out laughing, and his laughter infected all the others. He felt, at one and the same time, a sense of curiosity and a need: would his pee be equally invisible? And he carefully watered the rose bush with his urine and all he could see was the steam it gave off where it touched the earth. Their laughter was still echoing through the forest when the young woman moved. The roses had started to lose their petals in the breeze, then it was the turn of the more fragile stems. She crawled over to the old man. They helped each other up and, together, righted the cart; then the old man helped the young woman, who could barely walk, to lie down in the cart. The withered bush uprooted itself and tumbled away across the fields, carried by the now whistling wind. The old man began pulling the cart in fits and starts. When he was invisible, everything that was part of him was invisible too. The old man reached the road, where the going was easier. He followed the bush that was rustling along in the wind until it got caught on another bush beside the road. Lying in the cart, the young woman was singing softly, a song that tore at the old man's heart:

> I asked the river about my love
> the one who left so long ago,
> and for whom I'm dying of love, ai!

> I asked the river about my love,
> To tell me where he goes to bathe,
> and for whom I'm dying of love, ai!

The cart rolled along, and from it came a scent like that of the rose bush, only more acrid.

> The one who left so long ago
> and where he sadly bathed his lovely body,
> and for whom…

…and a sudden unexpected weight brought the cart to a halt. The young woman sat up, but could see no one. The old man, digging in his heels, began pulling again. She felt arms embracing her, lips pressed to her lips, and a body tenderly lay down beside her.

When the cart had passed, the withered rose bush detached itself from the other bush and was again carried off by the wind.

Araraquara, May 1964